# UNDERGROUND ESCAPADE

## A PETER AND MILLIE ADVENTURE

## SAM BARTRAM

ISBN: 979-8-65-703479-0

*For Ruth*

*My companion on many an escapade!*

# CHAPTER 1

"Somebody pinch me now!" I whispered, to nobody in particular. I immediately felt a sharp and painful pinch of my arm, just below the shoulder.

"Ouch!" I yelped, in a slightly more hushed tone than I would have done had I been literally anywhere else. "I sort of meant it figuratively! It wasn't an open invitation for an act of grievous bodily harm!"

"Sorry, I guess I'm a pretty literal person," Millie smiled back at me. "Anyway, that noise you made was pretty lame. You're such a wee softy!"

Carrying my bruised arm (and ego) with me, we began the long walk down probably the longest corridor I had ever had the opportunity to walk down. I say corridor – grand hall is probably a much better description. Seemingly following us with their eyes us as we walked were portraits of various Kings and Queens of the United Kingdom in all their regal splendour, dating back as far as anyone cared to remember.

"I could get used to this!" Millie whispered to me as we walked along. "My first trip to London is going to take some beating. This isnae a bad place! Nae too shabby!"

I chuckled to myself. That was some understatement

from Millie – we did in fact find ourselves in Buckingham Palace! Not too shabby indeed!

At this point, I should probably explain a little about who I am and what on earth my delightfully bonkers Scottish friend and I are doing at Buckingham Palace on a sunny Saturday in April. It's only polite after all!

My name is Peter Lipscombe and I'm a rather scrawny, plain-looking, normal kind of a boy from rural Cambridgeshire. I'd love to make myself sound more interesting than that, but I feel I owe you the truth if I want you to come on this journey with me! Don't get me wrong, scratch a little beneath the surface and I do have some redeeming qualities – my intelligence and undeniable athletic ability to name but a few! Even if I do say so myself!

Around ten months ago, my life changed forever when my best friend Finny sadly died. For a few months I felt bereft of purpose. I was totally inconsolable and refused to let the outside world in. However, a seemingly bizarre decision by my parents to take me on holiday to the ruggedly charming Scottish island of Orsk actually turned out to be a masterstroke, and slowly allowed me to see that I needed to start to live life again. Not just for me, but also for the life that my wonderful friend wasn't able to have himself.

The single most important person in regaining my *joie de vivre* was unquestionably Millie. Ah, the incomparable Millie McCluskey! I had met her on holiday in Orsk. She took it upon herself to show me the beauty of her beloved island and had, perhaps unknowingly, also reaffirmed to me the beauty of living. It may sound a little clichéd but we are all so lucky to be here on this earth. It's not always rainbows and butterflies but it's a pretty special place and we have to make the most of every second we have here - I'm now certain of it. Millie is the personification of this attitude. Confident, funny, kind, ballsy and just occasionally a little crazy, but always living her life to the maximum. She became an incredible friend in a very short period of time, and since my trip to Scotland we had spoken regularly on the phone and via WhatsApp. Oh, and did I mention she also helped me to uncover a huge international smuggling operation? You know, that old chestnut! More on that later…

Anyway, that brings us back to why we happened to find ourselves at Buckingham Palace. We were both there to collect a prestigious George Medal for our efforts in uncovering the criminal activity taking place on the Isle of Orsk, and helping to bring those responsible to justice. Millie had never been to England before and her parents had decided to take the opportunity to turn the visit into a holiday, accompanying my family on a trip to London for the weekend before staying with us in Cambridgeshire for the rest of the week.

To add to the excitement of seeing Millie after so long and meeting the Queen, it was to be a bumper weekend for me, as I had also managed to qualify for an inter-county Athletics finals at Crystal Palace National Sports Centre the following day. I was slightly disappointed to have not made the Cambridgeshire Under 15 team in my best event, the 800 metres, but a welcome consolation was a place in the 400-metre relay team. What a weekend in prospect!

"Ahem, listen up ladies and gentleman," boomed the voice of a very smartly dressed gentleman that greeted us at the end of the corridor. "Could Peter Lipscombe and Millie McCluskey please step forward?"

I looked across at Millie. She looked uncharacteristically nervous.

"Let's do this," I said to her, doing my best impression of sounding confident.

"Together," Millie responded with a smile.

We both walked forward to a slightly bemused look from the suited gentleman.

"Good morning children," the gentleman said. "Can I

just double check that you are Peter Lipscombe and Millie McCluskey? It says on my piece of paper that you helped to locate and bring down an international smuggling operation…"

"Yes, that's us," I confirmed. The gentleman clearly didn't think we looked capable of such a feat. I have to say, if I was him, I'd have been thinking exactly the same thing!

"Well, in that case – very well done indeed! Your country is proud of you! Now, follow me please," the gentleman enthused.

We walked through a little wooden door and along a much smaller wood-panelled corridor until we came to a larger door at the far end. We stopped at the door and the gentleman turned to talk to us.

"Alright, try not to be nervous. You are both here today because you have done something incredible and everyone here wants to congratulate you for that, including Her Majesty. When you go through this door you will need to face the audience. There are crosses marked on the floor for you to stand on, and there will be others receiving awards also. Line up next to them. There should only be a few minutes to wait before Her Majesty arrives. She will work her way along the line and will talk briefly to each person before presenting their medal. You must address her initially as 'Your Majesty' and then after that as 'Ma'am'. That's 'Ma'am' rhyming with jam, not rhyming with arm. Is that all understood?"

"Yes, that's fine," I replied. I looked over at Millie who looked as white as a sheet. Her complexion was pale at the best of times, but at this moment looked almost ghost-like.

"Millie, are you ok?" I asked.

"I'm a wee bit nervous," she managed to mutter. That was the understatement of the century! I was a little nervous but she did not look at all well.

"It'll be fine. She's just a little old lady really. Just pretend you're visiting your nan!" were my words of wisdom.

"My nanny certainly isnae the Queen though," was Millie's response. I couldn't really argue with that.

Just then the door opened and we were ushered through, taking up our positions by standing on the masking tape crosses on the floor. I looked out at the small crowd and could instantly pick out the faces of my mum and dad, beaming with pride. Dad offered a little wink of encouragement. My mum, not known for her subtlety, gave a huge double thumbs-up whilst grinning ear to ear like a Cheshire cat. So embarrassing! Mind you, it could have been worse. Millie's parents were dressed head to toe in tartan! Her father's outfit, complete with kilt, really was something to behold! At least they would be easy to spot if we got separated!

"Ladies and gentlemen, please be upstanding for Her Majesty, the Queen," boomed another suited gentleman – and there she was! Queen Elizabeth II herself, looking resplendent in a bright yellow coat and hat. As she walked along the line of people, gradually making her way towards us, I once again checked on Millie. She was now shaking a lot!

"What's the matter?" I whispered.

"I think I'm going to wee myself!" Millie replied rather too loudly, with a pained expression on her face.

"Please don't!" I replied. "Here comes the Queen…"

"Your Majesty, this is Millie McCluskey of Orsk in Scotland, and Peter Lipscombe of Little Dunham in Cambridgeshire," the suited gentleman said. "They are both receiving the George Medal for their part in helping uncover a significant smuggling operation in the Shetlands."

"Very impressive," responded the Queen. "How old are you both?"

"Your Majesty, we are both thirteen," I answered. I was so impressed that I had even managed to speak.

The Queen looked at Millie. "I hear that you even

managed to survive a plane crash. You must be a very resilient young lady. What was that like?"

Millie tried to speak. No words were coming out. Nothing at all. Time seemed to slow down at this point. Every second that went past seemed like an eternity. All I could think was 'say something, anything, please!' but no words left Millie's mouth. Then finally Millie's mouth opened. This was it.

"Jam!" Millie spluttered, and with that her whole body tensed up. A second later she slumped to the floor in a heap.

Oh my days!

# CHAPTER 2

"Where am I?" the dazed figure of Millie McCluskey asked, whilst slumped over a sort of chaise longue.

"You're at Buckingham Palace dear," Mrs McCluskey responded.

"Have we seen the Queen yet? Have we got our medals?" Millie enquired.

"Yes, here's your medal my love," Mr McCluskey said as he passed his daughter's medal to her.

"Wow, shiny!" Millie observed, somewhat stating the obvious. She sat up a little and spotted me stood behind her parents. "Peter, what happened? How did I do?"

What could I say in this situation? I thought it probably better to start with the truth.

"Well, there's some good news and some bad news. A couple of negative points – you called the Queen 'jam' and then fainted, almost squashing one of her corgis…"

"Oh dearie me!" Millie shrieked. "That's so embarrassing! What's the good news?"

"It was hilarious!" I shouted, and began howling with laughter. Millie scowled at me before slowly beginning to chuckle. Soon all of us were creased up with laughter.

"Well, I suppose at least the Queen is going to

remember me!" Millie eventually said.

"That she is, my wee girly, and no mistake," Mrs McCluskey said, whilst hugging her daughter tightly.

"Erm, not just the Queen," I added, looking at my new smartphone. "It appears that you have gone viral!"

I held out my phone whilst Millie, her parents, and mine crowded around. There was the video, already plastered all over social media. Incredibly within a few minutes it had already been viewed 300,000 times on YouTube. Millie's face had gone from pale white to bright crimson in a matter of moments.

"I always knew my wee girl would be famous!" Mr McCluskey chuckled.

Millie said nothing. We had inadvertently found out what it took to stop Millie from talking!

"Are you ok love?" my mum asked. "Don't listen to the boys. It must have been very nerve-wracking. I'm sure this sort of thing happens all the time, so don't worry."

Millie smiled. Mum had a knack of saying the right thing to make you feel better.

"You do look a wee bit red in the face my love," Mrs McCluskey commented.

"Yes, very red," I mischievously muttered. "Kind of like…jam!"

I'd gone too far. Millie sat up and started to lurch towards me. Sensing an impending wallop, I began to run! A sight not often seen in Buckingham Palace I imagine – two thirteen-year-olds chasing each other down the historic corridors. I hoped nobody had a camera phone to hand or I might be the next one going viral!

After Millie had run off her anger/embarrassment, we were politely escorted from the Palace by two more suited gentleman before reconvening outside the Palace gates at the top of the Mall. It was a lovely sunny day so we decided to find a nice spot for a picnic in St. James Park. We all had great glee in devouring the sandwiches that Mrs McCluskey had lovingly prepared the night before. I had secretly hoped for a McDonalds but at that very moment all was perfect.

We spent the rest of the afternoon sightseeing. We took a walk around the sights of central London, including a trip to the National Gallery. This was my dad's idea. I was not massively into Art, but even I was impressed by the big names on show. Monet, Van Gogh, Titian, Da Vinci – heavy hit after heavy hit!

"Oooh, Monet – I've heard of him!" Millie shouted out, drawing disapproving stares from the surrounding Art lovers.

"Not quite so loud Millie," I whispered to her. "People are trying to take it all in. Think library!"

"Ok, sorry. This isnae really my thing Peter," Millie replied, still probably slightly too loudly.

"Me neither," I said, "but I come to lots of these places with my parents. My dad is very into his Art".

"Oooh, look Van Gogh!" shouted Millie again. "Mr Lipscombe, is he the choppy ear man?"

Dad sighed gently, a little piece of him dying inside. I smiled at Millie. She was unashamedly Millie, and that was exactly who she should be.

After the gallery, my dad had a surprise.

"Right, time for a lovely slap-up meal! I'm paying!"

This was something particularly out of the ordinary. Dad was not known for his lavish gestures, and was rarely keen on parting with his hard-earned cash. It must be a special occasion!

We decided to return to our hotel, the illustrious Penge Travel Tavern, and eat somewhere near there so that we would not be too late to bed. It was my big race the following day after all.

"What's it to be then young people?" my mum asked. My eyes lit up and my mouth watered – I loved having the choice of where we went for a meal.

"Pasta or rice?" my dad said. "Got to get those carbs into your body. Plenty of energy for your big race!"

That limited our options a little more, but after much discussion, Millie and I settled on Indian cuisine. There were no Indian restaurants on her home island of Orsk, so she was really keen to enjoy some proper Indian food.

The Taj Mahal in Penge was an unusual place. I couldn't recall going to a restaurant before that had televisions on the walls. Literally everywhere. It wasn't like there was anything interesting on the televisions either. Just rolling news channels – BBC News, CNN, Sky News, Al Jazeera, Russia Today. All muted so the customers could fully enjoy the loud Indian pop music blaring out of surround sound speakers. It was certainly unlike anything I had experienced before.

"Indian cuisine and current affairs all under the same roof. What could be better?" my dad commented. I'm sorry to say he meant it as well – his personal heaven!

We all ordered. I decided to order the Chicken Korma as I thought I'd better avoid anything too spicy with my race the following day. Millie decided to test herself with a Lamb Madras. That's Millie for you - so competitive that she couldn't bear the idea of someone succeeding in consuming a spicier curry than her!

The food was absolutely delicious, and in spite of the 'interesting' décor, the evening was a lot of fun, with everyone in high spirits. The waiter had even asked Millie for her autograph, having recognised her from the now internationally infamous clip of her collapsing in front of the Queen. Millie was half way through writing her signature when she froze. She was completely motionless, with her emerald eyes as wide as saucers.

"Millie are you ok?" I asked.

Millie said nothing. She slowly lifted her finger and pointed behind me. I turned around to look at the television screen and my jaw dropped to the floor at the sight      of      the      face      on      screen.

# CHAPTER 3

The headline on the news channel in massive bold letters read 'JAILBREAK: SUSPECT AT LARGE'. Above the headline was a mugshot of a face Millie and I knew only too well. The mugshot belonged to career criminal Derek Mooney.

Millie and I had encountered Derek Mooney on the isle of Orsk, when he had been masquerading as a butler using the pseudonym 'De Mouney'. He was one of the gang on the island that had been involved in the smuggling of illegal pharmaceuticals into Britain. In the ensuing criminal investigation that our intervention had helped to bring about, it transpired that actually, far from being a lowly butler for the Baron of Orsk, he was in fact the head of operations for the criminal gang behind the smuggling. Conversely, the Baron, a strange individual who we were led to believe was some sort of mafia boss, had actually been somewhat coerced into becoming involved due to a myriad of financial difficulties, and his involvement stretched only to letting the gang have full use of his various properties. Something he probably regretted as he settled down to a good few years at her majesty's pleasure! Derek Mooney however, was seemingly a free man. How could this happen?

"Don't panic Millie, we'll find out what's going on," I said as I tried to reassure her. Inside though, I was panicking nearly as much as Millie. This was a very dangerous individual with a score to settle!

"What's the matter you two? You look like you've seen a ghost!" Dad commented.

"Dad, look!" I said, drawing his attention to the screen in front of us. Everyone else at the table also turned to look. There was a wide variety of different shocked faces – if someone had taken a picture of the table at that moment, it would have been a sight to behold.

"Well, that's put me off finishing my Lamb Bhuna!" exclaimed Mum.

The next few moments entailed everyone at the table googling away to try and find out more about what had happened. I settled on the BBC news article, and for whatever reason, I decided to read it out loud to the whole table:

NOTORIOUS CRIMINAL ON THE RUN AFTER PRISON VAN HIJACKING: Police are today searching for a dangerous criminal after a prison van transporting him was hijacked. Derek Mooney, 43, was being transferred to a prison with a higher security rating after a series of run-ins with fellow inmates. The incident, which is being described as highly organised and meticulously orchestrated, happened when the van stopped at a set of traffic lights. The hijackers, who were heavily armed, used a combination of explosives to blow a large hole in the side of the van before escaping with Mr Mooney in an unmarked white Ford Transit van. Mr Mooney has recently been convicted of several counts including smuggling, kidnapping, murder and attempted murder, and was two months into a life sentence. He has been described as extremely dangerous, most likely armed, and the general public are advised not to approach him if they see him, but instead to contact the police immediately. The police are also appealing for witnesses for the incident which occurred this afternoon in Buckinghamshire.

This all took a little while to sink in. After a few minutes we decided it would be a good idea to settle our bill and head to our hotel to contemplate this rather worrying news. We walked the few hundred metres to the hotel, where waiting for us in reception were two police officers, one male and one female.

"Mr and Mrs Lipscombe and Mr and Mrs McCluskey? Good evening. Could we please have a quiet word? Probably best to go up to your rooms," the female police officer said, conscious of the groups gathered in the hotel lobby, listening to their every word.

"It's Doctor Lipscombe actually," my dad responded, as if that was an important detail at this time! He always pulled up people who referred to him as Mr rather than Doctor. And it was always equally embarrassing. As if people are meant to know he's a doctor just by looking at him. I'm sorry – I know he worked hard at medical school and all that, but when he's not wearing his stethoscope, he's just another normal human being. I'm sure Mr would suffice right now! Don't tell him I said that though. I wouldn't want to pour water on his bonfire, as it were. Anyway, I digress…

"Ok, Doctor Lipscombe," the female police officer responded, sounding a little put out by my father's abruptness. "Do you mind showing us the way?"

All eight of us traipsed up the three flights of stairs to the level our rooms were on. The lift at the Penge Travel Tavern was unsurprising out of order, which was in keeping with the general atmosphere of the hotel. Dad led us all into our room, where the four parents sat on the edge of the double bed. Millie and I plonked ourselves on a small pull-out bed that I had already spent one uncomfortable night on. The male police officer sat on the room's single chair whilst the female police officer made herself comfortable by perching on the small table underneath the mirror.

"Right guys. I'm Sergeant Devonish. This is Officer Moore. We're from the Metropolitan Police," the male police officer began. "We just wanted to pay you a visit to reassure you about something you may have seen in the press today."

"So, you've come to tell us that the prison service hasn't let a dangerous criminal escape then?" chirped Millie. Wow, she was in a feisty mood. This was one of my favourite parts of having Millie as a friend. Just sit back and watch the fireworks!

"Well, err, no. But…" the poor police officer stuttered.

"So how exactly are we meant to feel reassured?" Millie continued.

"Well, err, it's just, erm…"

His lower-ranked colleague stepped in. "What Sergeant Devonish is trying to say, is that we can understand if you are worried about the events of today. We have our very best teams working around the clock to locate the whereabouts of Mr Mooney. We will find him and have him back behind bars as soon as we can."

"Please try not to worry," Sergeant Devonish said, finding his voice. "It is important to stress that we do not believe that any of you are in immediate danger. The very last place that Mr Mooney will travel to at this time will be London. He will be keeping a low profile in a rural location, and there is a suggestion that he may even be trying to return to Scotland. It makes no sense for him to come to London."

"Can you guarantee this though?" my dad asked. "Peter has a very important Athletics event tomorrow, but the most important thing is his safety. Should we be pulling him out of the event and going home?"

My heart sank. I had put everything into qualifying for this event. To run at the same track that the likes of Usain

Bolt and Michael Johnson had in the past. Surely I could just compete in my event and then return home? Like the police officer was saying, Mooney would be long gone by now. That being said, I've no doubt he would be the type to bear a grudge, and after Millie's spectacular collapse at Buckingham Palace he would know we were in London. Perhaps the risk of being caught would be too great?

"You can let the boy race," Sergeant Devonish replied. "We have direct assurances from the Commissioner of the Metropolitan Police that your safety will not be compromised in any way. Please carry on your business as usual. We will be in touch immediately if that situation changes. The Commissioner is not someone who risks her reputation with empty words, trust me!"

This was music to my ears at that moment. The show would go on!

The police officers carried on their conversation with our parents as they wandered towards the door of the room to be shown out. I turned to Millie who still looked a little concerned.

"Are you ok Mildred?" I asked. "You don't look too sure."

"I'm not sure why, but I've got a bad feeling about all this," Millie said.

"Look, I'll tell you what. I'll do my race tomorrow and then we'll head straight back to Cambridgeshire if that would make you feel better?" I offered up.

"Peter, I know what this race means to you. Let's just get it over with and get out of London," Millie blurted. "I'm not sure I can handle another adventure like last time."

"Thanks Millie," I said. I felt a little guilty but I was so in the zone. I had to be on that starting line tomorrow!

# CHAPTER 4

The one major positive about the action-packed day we'd just had (and the worrying news about Derek Mooney being on the run) was that I hadn't had time to get nervous about my race. I slept soundly – well, as soundly as could be hoped for, given the fact I was sleeping on the most uncomfortable bed in London!

I was rudely awoken by the incredibly annoying alarm tone I had set on my watch. It gradually got louder and lounder until it built up to a crescendo and I was forced to turn it off. 6am. Urgh!

"Morning love," shouted my mum, half-yawning as she stretched out her arms and clambered out of bed. "How are you feeling about your big race?"

"Ok, I think," I replied. "In the circumstances anyway."

"Try not to worry champ," my dad offered, as he sat up in bed. "The police were very clear that there is nothing to be worried about. This is the Met Police as well – they see a bit more of this stuff than we do in Little Dunham!"

Well that was true enough, but wasn't saying a great deal. The most exciting thing to ever happen in our village was when a large Lorry tried to go underneath the old railway bridge and got wedged underneath. It was stuck there for a week whilst they tried to figure out a way of removing it. This was in 1978 and people still talk about it! That's village life for you! Nonetheless, Dad seemed confident enough that things would be alright, which certainly helped my mood.

We met the McCluskeys for breakfast in the less than welcoming cafeteria area of the Penge Travel Tavern. Fortunately, the breakfast looked more appealing than the décor. I looked on slightly enviously at the large fried breakfasts that everyone else was wolfing down. My breakfast consisted of one slice of toast and one large bowl of muesli with skimmed milk. Not exactly heaven for the taste buds, but I had bigger fish (or bacon!) to fry – out on the track.

It was a short walk to the Crystal Palace National Sport Centre. I had arranged to meet the rest of the relay team outside the stadium and then to go in together. I was the first one there – this was typical of my dad's timekeeping. We were always early for everything – usually hours early!

"It's ok guys, you can go in and find your seats. I'll wait here for the boys," I said.

"It's nae bother. I'll wait with you. I'm looking forward to meeting your wee pals," Millie replied. That was nice of her. I was glad of the company as there was still a little while to wait. My parents and Millie's folks left us to find their seats, whilst Millie and I perched ourselves on a grassy bank. After a few minutes of chatting I heard some familiar voices.

"There he is. The national treasure!"

We turned around, and there they were – the rest of the Cambridgeshire Under 15 relay team. Usually my rivals in the big County competitions, today they were to be my team mates. There was Paul Baker from Soham – he was a quiet chap but a fearsome competitor. He was the shortest member of the team and stood out for his rather severe haircut. He shaved his head every day as he believed it made him more aerodynamic and gained him crucial seconds! No stone was left unturned in his pursuit of athletic excellence, despite perhaps not being the most naturally gifted of the bunch.

Stood next to Paul was the tall figure of Alfie Johnson, who hailed from Ely. Alfie's running style was ungainly but effective, his long limbs eating up the ground at a rapid pace. He was not the most stylish, but I got the impression that he didn't really care. Either that or was blissfully unaware! His hairstyle could best be described as a 'pudding bowl' – yes, curtains were alive and well in Cambridgeshire! He was a friendly and cheerful boy though, and it was always a pleasure to be in his company.

That left the incomparable Du'ane Joseph. Without question the superstar of our team and almost certainly a future star of British Athletics. Du'ane's grandfather was a sprint legend in his home country of Antigua and had been a gold medallist at the Antiguan National Championships on a number of occasions. Athletics was in his blood, and he was as natural a talent as you could ever hope to find. Du'ane had already won the individual 200 metre and 400 metre events held over the past few days and was counting on us to deliver the goods to complete his gold medal haul.

"Good morning Lippy," Du'ane said as he approached. I've no idea why he called me that but I hated it! "I hear congratulations are in order. Sorry I missed your medal ceremony with the Queen yesterday but I was a little busy collecting a medal or two of my own!"

"Well done mate," I replied with a genuine warmth. I am competitive, but where it comes to Du'ane there was just no competition. He was totally different class. In fact, Du'ane was pretty much perfect in every way. A good-looking lad of mixed Caribbean and White British descent, his beautifully maintained afro was the envy of the rest of the East Anglian athletics fraternity. Needless to say, he also seemed hugely popular with the girls and usually attracted a large fan club to his races.

His home life was seemingly idyllic too. He lived in a huge historical house right in the centre of Cambridge near many of the University buildings. His mother was a professor of biology at Cambridge University itself and was world famous in her field, whilst his father was an infographics expert that worked for the BBC in London. I found myself wanting to hate him, I really did, but unfortunately, he was just such a good guy it was virtually impossible to do. I just had to accept that I was yet another paid-up member of the Du'ane Joseph fan club!

"You must be the famous Millie McCluskey," Du'ane said, turning his attention to Millie. "Peter's told us so much about you. He didn't mention how beautiful you were though. Are all the girls from your island as lovely as you?"

Millie blushed a little and smiled back at Du'ane. "Thank you. You're nae so bad yourself".

I looked on at this exchange with a mixture of befuddlement and horror. What was happening here? I mean, Du'ane trying his cheesy lines was nothing new, but Millie flirting back? This truly disturbing scene of two worlds colliding was not going to plan!

Was I jealous? Millie and I had shared a kiss before – but that was when we were trapped underground and thought we may never escape. I didn't think of Millie in that way, did I? For whatever reason though, I did feel that this exchange needed to come to an abrupt halt.

"Millie, I think we'd better join up with the rest of our team and start warming up," I suddenly blurted, knowing well we actually had plenty of time.

"I guess so…" Millie responded after a brief pause, sounding a little hurt by my sudden desire to get rid of her. "I'll see you guys later, hopefully with a gold medal around your necks".

As Millie wandered off to find her parents, Du'ane turned to me and said, "That was a little uncalled-for man! Look - if you two are a thing then I'm not going to get in the way of that! I just like her style! Kind of feisty I reckon!"

"We're not a thing!" I responded, slightly flustered. "Anyway, what was with all of that cheesiness?"

"Sorry man. Look, I'll tone it down with Millie if that's what you want. Ok?" Du'ane replied. I nodded back in acknowledgement. The four of us made our way silently towards the stadium, the mood slightly tenser than it had been before this little exchange.

As we waited in line to be let in through the athletes' entrance, I broke the silence. "Are we ok Du'ane? Sorry about that. I don't know why I reacted like that."

"We're cool Lippy! No stress. Anyway, I'm not sure it's me you need to be apologising to – you need be saying sorry to that pretty friend of yours!" Du'ane replied with a glint in his eye. Now he was on the wind-up. He just couldn't help himself. I gave him a sharp, much-deserved punch in the arm. We smiled at each other. Everything was back to normal. Boys are simple creatures sometimes – even me, and I'm a cut above most of them!

Now, race time!

# CHAPTER 5

There is usually quite a lot of hanging about at an athletics meet and this was no different, albeit we were quite lucky in the scheduling of our event. The schedule for the day was that our semi-final was the very first race and if we qualified, the final would take place at around 2pm. We stretched and warmed up for a little while before being led out into the stadium for the race.

I looked around in the crowd and spotted my family, Millie, and the McCluskeys. I waved to them and couldn't help smiling from ear to ear. I was nervous, but more than anything I was proud to be competing in the event and so pleased that my best friend Millie was there to support me.

In the 4 x 400 metre relay, everyone who is going to be in the race (32 people) all start off by standing just next to the start line, so there is a lot of hustle and bustle, with teams having a last-minute huddle and pep talk. The first leg runners then make their way to their starting positions. For us this was going to be Paul, who would hopefully get us off to a blistering start. Paul was especially good at running in lanes, which is so important for the first leg of a 4 x 400 metre relay. He would be passing the baton to Alfie for the second leg, with me running the third leg. I was much more of an endurance athlete, so this suited me well – the hope being that I could hold my form and pass on to Du'ane for the all-important final leg. If we were anywhere near the leader at this stage, Du'ane would usually annihilate the opposition.

As Paul wandered over to the starting blocks, Du'ane leaned over to me. "How are you feeling Lippy? Nerves holding up ok?"

"Fine thanks," I replied. That was the truth as well. After being trapped underground and trying to outrun a gang of hardened criminals, I didn't seem to get as nervous about things like running races!

"Good to hear it my man," said Du'ane. "Just get that baton round to me, and I'll do the rest!"

I had one more look round to where Millie was sat. She smiled and waved. That was a good sign – I'd been worried that I may have offended her earlier, but she seemed ok. Phew!

The crowd hushed as they awaited the starting pistol. BANG! The first leg runners were off! Paul had made a flying start running in the tricky lane eight, but I was concerned he had gone off too quickly. In lane eight you can't see any of the other athletes so you just have to trust your form and try and pace it as best you can. Paul had not done a great job, and was down in about sixth place as he handed over to Alfie. The big man instantly made up some ground and by the time the lanes merged, his long limbs had carried us into around fourth position. Alfie decided to go around the outside on the final bend which proved to be a brilliant decision as he passed the baton to me in third place.

I kept my eyes focused on the runner from Kent in second place as I bounded around the first bend. Lancashire were a long way ahead in first place, so my target was to try and outlast the Kent athlete and give Du'ane a fighting chance of winning, and therefore being given the best lane draw for the final. I was just sitting on the shoulder of the Kentish athlete waiting for him to tire. Thankfully he couldn't keep up as I kicked for the line and passed the baton to Du'ane in an impressive, but distant, second place. The final lap was pure theatre. I watched from just beyond the finish line as Du'ane ate up the ground on the Lancastrian in first place. Twenty metres became ten metres. Ten metres became five metres. Coming into the final straight about two metres behind, there was only going to be one winner. Du'ane powered for the line, leaving his competitor floundering in his slipstream! An epic victory for Cambridgeshire! A team effort no doubt, but unquestionably the hero of the hour was Du'ane. We were into the final – as winners!

"Yes, you did it!" we all shouted to Du'ane as we embraced in a jubilant team huddle.

"*We* did it man! *We* did it! Get in there!" Du'ane shouted in response.

We walked around the outside of the track to celebrate our success with our families and friends. My mum and dad gave me a huge sweaty hug.

"Well done boy! You must focus again now though. Only half the job complete," was my dad's offering. This was typical Dad. Thankfully Millie was more enthusiastic.

"Wow! You guys were epic! I didnae know you were *that* good Peter! Very impressive!" she said, giving me a big hug.

"Thanks Millie," I said with a big grin on my face. Getting that compliment from Millie meant probably as much to me as winning. Compliments were not really her style usually, so I must have done something pretty special!

After a few minutes, Du'ane wandered over from where his parents were, to sit with Millie and I.

"Hi Du'ane," Millie said. "You were great! Well done! I'm looking forward to the final later."

"Thanks Millie. I enjoyed that too. For some reason it always seems more exciting to win a team event. It's fun to be able to celebrate with great guys like these," Du'ane said whilst putting his arm around me. "Look man, me and my parents are staying in this absolutely epic apartment at the moment overlooking Trafalgar Square. My dad is staying in London for work next week, so the BBC have let us stay in this place. They must own it I guess, but I'm telling you, it's ridiculous! There's even a pool table and a cinema-size television! It's sick! I've asked my dad and he says you two can stay with us tonight and travel back to Cambridge with my mum tomorrow if you want? There's plenty of room. Go on, we can celebrate our win in style!"

"Sign me up!" I said instantly, in that moment forgetting all about Derek Mooney and my previous agreement with Millie to go home straight after the race.

"Yes, that's my boy!" shouted Du'ane. "You cool with this too Millie?"

I guess Millie hadn't forgotten about Derek Mooney. How could she? After all, she was the one who had been kidnapped by him, not me.

"Erm, I'm not sure. Peter, I thought we were heading back after the race?" Millie said, nudging me sharply in the ribs.

"Well look, no pressure," said Du'ane. "Just let me know later yeah?" With that Du'ane headed back to sit with his family.

"Sorry Millie, I was so caught up with the race that I forgot all about everything else," I said.

"Now I feel bad Peter. I could see how excited you were. I'm just scared. I'd rather not take any chances, even if Du'ane's flat does sound really cool," Millie replied. "Do you understand?"

Of course I did, but I can't say I wasn't disappointed.

"It's fine Millie. Don't worry, we'll head back home afterwards as planned," I said.

"Thanks Peter. You're a great friend," Millie beamed.

We sat together watching the rest of the morning's races. I was so pleased with my day so far, but was now focusing on the final to come.

# CHAPTER 6

Our great local rivals Suffolk had also made it through to the final, which gave us even more reason to be excited about the race. I munched my way through a couple of energy bars to tide me over. Then an announcement!

"Can the athletes competing in the Under 15 boys 400 metre relay final please make their way to the start?"

This was it!

"Good luck Peter," said Millie. "You can do it!"

"Thanks," I hurriedly replied, and smiled back at Millie as I hastily made my way to the area near the start line where the athletes were gathering. Du'ane was looking his usual confident self, but Alfie and Paul were looking a little on edge. As we completed our usual pre-race ritual of gathering in a huddle, Du'ane was the one offering the motivational speech.

"Ok boys, this is it! In a few minutes we can be national county champions. There's no need to be nervous though. This is everything you've trained for. Just go out there and do what you can do. If we can repeat our run from the semi-final, we've got a great chance," Du'ane exclaimed, getting more animated with every word. His words seemed to have had the desired effect on Paul, who bounded over towards the starting blocks to await the gun.

The lane order for the final had been drawn earlier and was then announced over the booming sound system: "IN LANE ONE – KENT. LANE 2 – SUFFOLK. LANE 3 – LANCASHIRE. LANE 4 – CAMBRIDGESHIRE. LANE 5 – SOUTH YORKSHIRE. LANE 6 – SURREY. LANE 7 – WARWICKSHIRE. AND FINALLY, IN LANE 8 – DERBYSHIRE."

This time the silence was so absolute it was deafening. You could hear a pin drop as Paul got into position in his blocks. I could feel my heart beating faster and faster in my chest. Boom. Boom. Boom. BANG! The starter's pistol fired and off flew Paul! The final was underway and this time Paul had made an incredible start. He was almost level with the athlete from South Yorkshire by the second bend.

"Go Paul!" I shouted almost involuntarily, as he somehow produced the lap of his life to hand over to Alfie in a clear first place.

As Alfie sped off in his languid but effective style, I made my way onto the track to get into position to receive the baton. I'm not sure exactly why, but I decided at that moment to take a look at the crowd. I spotted Millie and my parents and waved, though their focus was entirely on Alfie as he powered along the back straight, maintaining our position in the lead of the race. My eyes scanned along the crowd. I couldn't believe I was about to race in a final in front of all these people. What a feeling!

As Alfie made his way around the final bend, I glanced for one final time at the jubilant spectators. Strangely there was one man that wasn't cheering and getting excited like the others. As my eyes focused in on him, I could see he was staring directly at me. He looked familiar. Wait a minute, he looked just like…no, it couldn't be…could it? It was! It was Derek Mooney!

I looked away for a second and rubbed my eyes. I looked back at where the man was stood. He was no longer there! Were my eyes playing tricks on me? They must be, I reasoned. That can't have been him. No chance! Unfortunately, by now my concentration and focus was completely gone. I looked behind me and approaching at great speed was Alfie – in first place! I began to run in order to receive the baton – but I had gone too late! Alfie was going to have to slow right down to pass the baton to me. The other teams were rapidly catching us. I reached out to grab the baton as Alfie forcefully placed it into the palm of my right hand. I grabbed it but not quite tightly enough and as my hand moved forward the baton was launched through the air. It almost flew in slow motion as I made a futile attempt to take it back under my grasp.

SLAM! The baton hit the floor and with it our chances of winning the race! I crumpled to the floor with my hands covering my face in shame.

The agony was almost too much to bear. Our dream of winning that gold medal was gone. Shattered. Extinguished. And the very worst part was that it was all my fault! Paul and Alfie had just run lifetime best performances. Du'ane hadn't even got to display his considerable athletic prowess, and could no longer complete his coveted hat-trick of gold medals. Tears very quickly began streaming down my face as I wandered slowly from the track, carrying the baton that I had retrieved after dropping it so clumsily. Nothing could make me feel any worse at this moment. Paul and Alfie were however going to try.

"Peter! You absolute muppet! We had that in the bag until you fumbled away our chances!" Paul shouted angrily.

With that, he turned and carried on walking past us. I turned to Alfie, hoping for a slightly more sympathetic response. Alfie was usually a friendly and caring sort, but the emotion of the occasion had got the better of him.

"Peter, I know you didn't mean it and everything, but I'm still so angry with you! You completely messed that up! What were you thinking? You started running far too late!" Alfie spluttered, in a softer tone than Paul but almost equally as critical.

I thought for a moment. I couldn't tell them the truth – that I may, or may not, have seen notorious criminal and prison escapee Derek Mooney. If it was him, which I had by now assured myself that it almost certainly wasn't and it was some sort of trick of the mind, then I would just panic everyone – especially Millie.

"I…I'm not sure," I stuttered. "It was just a mistake. I'm sorry."

"Not as sorry as I am, believe me!" Alfie replied, before wandering off to catch up with Paul, leaving just Du'ane and I standing together.

"I'm so sorry Du'ane," I began. "I stopped you from getting your third gold. You deserved to win more than anyone."

To my surprise and amazement, Du'ane responded calmly, "Never mind, these things happen. It's just a mistake. It could have happened to any of us. Yes, I'm disappointed, but there will be other races. We win as a team and lose as a team." With that, he gave me a huge hug. In that one moment, Du'ane had shown me the difference between a great athlete and a great sportsman. Putting to one side his personal disappointment to commiserate with his teammate and friend. What a guy!

At that moment, a third person joined the hug. "Urgh, you guys are well sweaty!"

It was of course Millie! I couldn't help but giggle a little. She always seemed to have that effect on me.

"I'm so sorry you didnae win guys! It was fun watching yous today anyway. Yous are all so fast I cannae believe it!" Millie said, clearly trying to make us feel better.

"Thanks Millie," I replied. "Thanks for coming along to watch. It meant a lot to have you here."

Just then, Du'ane's parents appeared and gestured at him to go over to them.

"Guys, I've got to head now. My dad has to do some

work over at the apartment," Du'ane explained. "It was nice to meet you Millie. Sorry about my cheesy lines earlier. I mean, it was all true, but I didn't mean to embarrass you!"

"Nae worries," Millie replied, smiling back at Du'ane.

"Look, I know we didn't win, but did you two want to come over and check out the apartment later? The offer still stands. My mum is more than happy to take you back home tomorrow," Du'ane asked.

"We'd love to!" said Millie, to my surprise and amazement.

"Great stuff!" exclaimed Du'ane. "I'll text the address to you. Come over whenever you're ready."

As Du'ane headed off towards his parents I looked at Millie with a slightly puzzled expression.

"I thought you wanted to go home straight way?" I queried.

"Aye, I did," replied Millie. "But you just looked really sad, with your wee sad little eyes. So, I had a rethink, and thought this might cheer you up."

Millie was amazing! The best! I did really want to check out the cool pad that Du'ane was staying in, however in the back of my mind I had a nagging doubt. Was the man in the crowd Derek Mooney? If it was, were we in danger? Should I tell Millie? I decided after pondering for a few seconds that the answer to all three of those questions was a resounding 'no', particularly if that meant a cool night in a swanky central London apartment!

"Millie, you are the best friend anyone could have!" I said, smiling back at her. I meant it too.

"Aye, that I am Peter Lipscombe! Don't you forget it!" Millie replied with one of her glorious freckly smiles.

# CHAPTER 7

My parents took some convincing to allow us to go to Du'ane's apartment.

"I'm really not sure love. The last time you and Millie went a-wandering, it ended up with you being trapped underground and Millie being kidnapped. Oh, and a plane crash!" exclaimed Mum.

"Well, when you put it like that it doesn't sound great!" I replied, with some degree of understatement. "But this is different. We are just staying at a friend's house overnight. With Mr and Mrs Joseph there – who you know, and trust. It's risk free!"

"Risk free – apart from the fact that there is a hardened criminal on the loose, with every reason to want to come looking for you," Dad chipped in.

"You heard what the police officers said," I replied. "Mooney is never going to take the chance of coming into London when he knows the world and his wife are looking for him."

As I said this, I thought again about the man I had seen in the crowd. By this time, I had come to the conclusion it was some sort of hallucination, brought about by a combination of extreme nerves about the race and perhaps one too many energy drinks! There may have been someone vaguely resembling Derek Mooney in the crowd, but it was doubtful that the man himself would prioritise an inter-county athletics competition over avoiding being caught by the police!

"Peter, we'll have to discuss this with Millie's parents. After all, it was Millie that ended up being kidnapped by Mooney up in Scotland." This was my dad's final word on the matter. He could be quite authoritative when he wanted to be. Or at least give that impression.

Millie and I watched from a few metres away as my parents and the McCluskeys had a brief conference on the matter. After a couple of minutes, we were summoned over.

"We have decided that you can go to your friend's house…" Mr McCluskey began.

"Yes!" Millie and I shouted in unison, exchanging a slightly ungainly high five!

"…but you will text all of us on the hour, every hour, as well as before you go to sleep and when you wake up. That might seem over-protective, but we nearly lost you both once and we can't risk that again. Do you understand?" Mr McCluskey continued.

"Yes, we understand," we chirped in unison, barely containing the excitement on our faces. This was going to be fun!

I quickly got changed and then we immediately began the short walk to Crystal Palace train station. At the station, we stood for far longer than was absolutely necessary in front of a large map of the London transport network, trying to figure out the routes that we needed to take. Six 'out of towners' in the big city! After much discussion, my dad described in an extremely long-winded and overly verbose manner exactly which route we needed to take.

"Right, first we all have to board the train towards central London. Then at Canada Water, you two must alight the train and board the Docklands Light Railway heading westbound. Then when you reach Waterloo station, you can board the Northern Line heading in a northbound direction before coming to your final stop at Charing Cross Station," Dad explained.

"Dad, I'm sure we can read the underground map," I replied. Sensing my dad looking slightly crestfallen at my mockery of his lengthy description, I added, "Thank you for your help though."

The train soon arrived and on we clambered. It was seven stops before we arrived at Canada Water, and the journey seemed to drag a little. I was desperate by this point to shed our parents, and begin our own exploration of London. As the train arrived at Canada Water station, not too far from London's world-renowned financial district, we said our goodbyes to our parents. A couple of hugs and a few renditions of 'see you tomorrow' and 'be careful' later, we hopped off the train, looking forward to doing something we had never done before – exploring the big city on our own!

As expected, we had no problems finding our way onto the correct train. As we settled into our seats on a relatively quiet carriage, all thoughts of the disappointment of dropping the baton had faded into the background. My focus was now totally on looking ahead – and having a great night in a lavish apartment overlooking Trafalgar Square!

I looked over at Millie. She was looking around, almost in wonderment. I always loved visiting London, but to Millie, this was a whole new world. She had never been outside of Scotland before, and London was proving a real culture shock.

"Are you ok Millie?" I asked, as it was unlike her to be quiet for this length of time!

"Aye, I'm grand thank you," Millie replied. "I just love looking around at everyone and imagining what their lives are like. How did they get here? Where are they off to? I bet everyone on this carriage has an interesting story to tell. It must be interesting to live in London."

"I thought you wouldn't swap the Isle of Orsk for anything?" I queried.

"Well, Orsk is my home. I've never really thought about living anywhere else before. Just being here though – the sights, the sounds, the bright lights, all the different interesting people. I mean…it's really something!" Millie reflected.

I could almost see the change in Millie happening before my eyes. Whenever we had spoken about London before, she had described it as 'everything that is wrong about the modern world' – with its noise, pollution, overcrowding and the like. However, even Millie had to admit that London town had a bewitching effect on her – the atmosphere was intoxicating and almost against her will, she kept wanting more and more.

Before we knew it, we had arrived at the world-famous Waterloo Station.

"Right, now we need to find the platform for the Northern Line," I stated, whilst gazing at my pocket map of the underground network.

"Ok," replied Millie, "but first can I get a photo in the main hall, near that big clock!"

"Millie! It's a train station! It's where people travel through to get to the places that are worth taking a photo of!" I laughed.

"To you maybe!" Millie replied, acknowledging my gentle teasing with a smile. "But where I come from, we don't even have a railway line! This station is probably the size of the whole of Orsk village! It's pretty incredible! Come on – one quick photo and we'll be on our way."

How could I refuse? Millie had kindly taken me under her wing to show me around her island when I was so sad after the death of my best friend Finny. I owed her so much.

"Go on then!" I relented. "Let's make it quick though –

I'm desperate to see Du'ane's pad!"

As requested, we made our way into the large main hall, near the huge clock. In fairness to Millie, had I never seen a station of this size before, I would probably have been equally impressed. My dad would probably describe it as a 'remarkable example of Victorian architectural engineering' or some such phrase.

"Right, where do you want to stand?" I asked Millie. "Do you want the clock in the background?"

"Yes please, and that big sign that says Waterloo Station," Millie replied.

I took out my phone to line up the shot. Millie looked very photogenic with her distinctive long, curly red hair. During our trip to the National Gallery the day before, my dad had made some comment about Millie looking like a pre-Raphaelite muse. I presumed that to be some kind of nerdy compliment! If so, it was certainly warranted.

Just then, I noticed a figure moving around in the background. Although clearly Waterloo is a busy station, with more important things going on than our photograph, this person was somewhat ruining the shot! I waited a few moments for them to move past, but instead they gradually walked closer and closer. The 'photo bomber' was wearing a hoodie so it was hard to tell whether it was a man or a woman at first, but either way, they clearly did not want us to take our photograph!

All of a sudden, the hooded figure sprinted towards Millie, grabbing her tightly around the waist. Out of complete shock, Millie instinctively kicked the figure hard in the right shin, causing them to relinquish their grasp and at the same time causing their hood to fly back, revealing their face. This time there was no mistaking who it was.

At the top of my voice I shouted, "MILLIE! RUN! IT'S DEREK MOONEY!"

# CHAPTER 8

Millie and I sprinted as fast as our legs could take us. My athletic training meant that I was the faster runner but Millie was no slouch, and as we raced across the vast station hall, we gradually pulled away from the stumpy middle-aged criminal with a chip on his shoulder. It was hard to process everything that was going on due to the shock and having to think on our feet, but it was clear that Mooney was hell-bent on revenge.

"Where should we run to Peter?" Millie shouted breathlessly as we slalomed in and out of the crowds. "What should we do?"

I needed to think, and think quickly!

"Let's head for the Northern Line!" I panted in reply. "Du'ane's apartment is the safest place we could be at the moment. Hopefully we can time it perfectly and jump on a train just as it's leaving. We could lose Mooney that way."

We continued running as fast as we could towards the underground platforms. As we turned a corner, I glanced out of the corner of my eye to see how far away Mooney was. We had gained fifteen metres or so, but he was still hot on our tail. Just ahead I spotted the ticket barriers fast approaching.

"How's your hurdling?" I asked Millie.

"Not sure!" she replied in haste.

"Well we're about to find out! I want you to jump the barriers!" I blurted.

With that we picked out two barriers without a queue and almost simultaneously leaped – and cleared them comfortably!

"Oi!" shouted an angry gentleman, presumably someone who worked for Transport for London. There was no chance of him catching us though! We were gone!

As we came to a long escalator, we sprinted down the left-hand side, carefully avoiding the long line of commuters positioned to the right. Millie had a brief opportunity to look behind as we descended.

"Mooney is still following! He's not far behind!" Millie screamed exasperatedly.

"Ok!" I shouted. "When we get to the bottom, look both ways and sprint to catch whichever train is about to leave. It doesn't matter if it's going the wrong way – we can change at the next station. Now when I count to three, copy what I do! Ready – one, two, three!"

With that, I leapt up on the metal partition between the escalators, and began to slide down on my bottom! It was something I'd always wanted to do, but had no idea if it actually worked – but, boy, did it work! It must have been some sight to behold – Millie and I zooming down this oversized slide! It was very dangerous, definitely not allowed and probably illegal, but preferable to being caught by Mooney!

As we flew off at the bottom, we landed together in a crumpled heap. We quickly dusted ourselves off and looked to the platforms either side. We were in luck! A train was sat there ready to leave, and it was heading northbound. Without a second's hesitation we sprinted for the doors. We had made it!

"Come on doors! Close! Close now!" Millie whispered out loud. My heart was pounding and felt like it was going to leap out of my chest.

Just then Mooney appeared, looking a little the worse for wear! He charged at the train heading for the next set of doors to where we were stood! He hadn't seen us get on, but had guessed that we would be on the train! Oh no! The doors closed, but by this time our view was obscured and we couldn't see whether Mooney had made it onto the train or not.

As we began moving, I had a brainwave! I spotted a group of what I presumed to be university students, in full fancy dress costume as the rock band Queen.

"Wow, I love your outfits guys!" I said enthusiastically.

"Cheers fella!" shouted the young man dressed as Brian May, greeting our praise with a thumbs-up.

"Do you mind if we quickly try on your jackets and wigs?" I asked.

Millie looked at me strangely for a second, before seemingly twigging what I was up to.

"Don't see why not," the man obligingly replied.

A few seconds later Derek Mooney walked along the carriage, and despite looking directly at us, walked straight through. In fairness he probably wasn't expecting to find us moonlighting as Freddie Mercury and Brian May!

"Phew!" exclaimed Millie, breathing a large sigh of relief as she subtly peeled off the fake moustache. "That was a genius idea Peter. I never would have thought of that."

"I'm not sure where that came from!" I replied. "What a close shave! No moustache pun intended…"

We sat tight for a little while, hoping that we would spot Mooney leave the train at the next station, Embankment. We couldn't see him so we presumed that he was still on the train.

"The next stop is our stop," I said to Millie. "I think our best bet is to get off the train and try and blend into the crowd. If Mooney gets off as well, we may need to try and hide for a little while. Let's stay together and hope for the best!"

"Ok Peter," Millie responded. "I trust you."

At this point I felt a pang of guilt. I should have mentioned seeing Mooney in the crowd at the stadium. Perhaps I would tell Millie later. Thinking about it now, it must have been him watching me at Crystal Palace. He would probably have been following us all day before deciding to approach us at Waterloo Station. That seemed like a strange decision – to attack someone in broad daylight in front of a huge crowd of commuters and tourists. He was obviously not thinking straight, and if anything, that made him even more dangerous.

Anyway, no time to think about that now. The train slowly ground to a halt at Charing Cross station and we readied ourselves to disembark.

"Ready?" I asked.

"As I'll ever be," Millie responded.

As we alighted the carriage, I immediately spotted Mooney coming out of another set of doors further down the carriage.

"Quick, bob down slightly and keep moving," I hastily uttered. "Mooney has stepped off the train."

We quickly scuttled over to near the escalator. Ensuring that we were both hidden from view, we peered back at the platform. The platform was now more or less empty, bar a couple of stragglers who had just missed the last train. Mooney stood there for a few seconds looking lost. He was gazing up and down the platform.

"Do you think he's looking around for us?" Millie whispered.

"You'd have to guess so. Don't worry, he can't see us here. We're out of his field of vision. Even if he does spot us, we are right next to the escalator so can make a move quickly," I quietly muttered, offering Millie some reassurance.

Just then it appeared to dawn on Mooney that he had lost us. He walked up to the nearest wall and screamed!

"AAARRRGGGHHH!" he yelled, as he punched the wall with considerable force.

"Wow! He isnae happy, is he?" Millie commented.

"That's an understatement I'd say," I remarked, smiling at Millie.

"It's kind of like watching the gorilla enclosure at a zoo," Millie said, smiling back.

The people on the platform had wisely moved away from Mooney, who had gone to sit on a bench, presumably waiting for the next train.

"I think he's given up on looking for us," said Millie.

"It looks like it," I replied. "Let's watch him for another minute or two, and then when he gets on the train, we'll go to the police."

The next train arrived and the platform emptied, leaving the solitary figure of Derek Mooney sitting there.

"What is he waiting for?" Millie asked. "He's behaving very oddly, isn't he?"

"None of it seems to make sense," I agreed.

"Perhaps we should head off now," Millie mooted. "Maybe the police can catch him before he leaves the platform."

As soon as the words left her mouth, Derek Mooney stood up and looked around suspiciously, as if to check he wasn't being watched. Then, he turned and began to walk quickly in the opposite direction to the escalator.

"Where's he going?" I thought out loud. I had the sudden thought to film whatever happened next with my new camera phone, in case I needed the evidence.

Mooney walked until he was at the very far end of the platform and came to a door. The door looked as though it led to a store cupboard. Mooney stopped and took another look around. Then he put his finger up towards something that from our now considerable distance looked like a bell. He pressed the 'bell' several times and then hastily pulled open the door and disappeared within!

Where            was            he            going?

# CHAPTER 9

As we slowly wandered over to the door that Derek Mooney had mysteriously disappeared into, I could feel a familiar sensation in the pit of my stomach. It was similar to how I'd felt last summer on the Isle of Orsk, when a determination to get to the truth took control of my senses. It was like an instinct that I couldn't help but act upon. The logical thing would be to get out of there and call the police. However, logic had been put to one side – at least temporarily.

We approached the door and noticed that the 'bell' had in fact been a combination lock. Whatever was beyond the door was something that was intended to remain secret.

"Well that's that then!" I huffed. "This mystery shall remain unsolved!"

"I do have a wee idea," Millie said. "Could I have a look at the video that you recorded on your phone?"

"Be my guest!" I replied.

I held out the phone and we watched the footage of Mooney skulking along the platform before disappearing through the door.

"Can I see the part where he taps the code into the combination lock again?" Millie asked.

"Ok. I'll pass you the phone so you can look closely," I replied.

Millie played the video to herself a few times.

"Peter, look at this," she said, showing me what she'd found out. "You can see how many times Mooney taps the wee keypad. Here we go – one, two, three, four and five! So, it's a five-digit combination we're looking for!"

"That's awesome. Well done!" I enthusiastically responded. "Although, that still means that there are ten thousand different combinations."

"That's right. The thing is, I have an idea of what the combination might be, based on which row of numbers he taps on. Look – you can kind of see!" Millie continued.

Millie was right. If you paused and zoomed in, you could see if he was pressing a number higher or lower on the keypad. Not the exact row, but a starting point.

"Nice work!" I commented. "It's still going to be like finding a needle in a haystack though."

"Peter, try this number – 01806 – give it a try! Go on!" Millie instructed, getting gradually more and more animated.

I hurriedly tapped the number into the keypad and attempted to turn the handle. To my shock and surprise, the door swung open!

"But...how...what?" I stuttered in amazement.

"I cannae believe it! It was just a guess really!" Millie excitedly replied.

"Why that number?" I asked, still puzzled at our unlikely first-time success.

"It's the telephone area code for the Isle of Orsk!" Millie blurted. "Whatever your view of the place it leaves an impression on you!"

I couldn't disagree. It's an amazing place! And more importantly it spawned at least one incredible human being – Millie McCluskey, take a bow! Since meeting her, Millie had never ceased to amaze me – tour guide, grief counsellor, private detective and now puzzle queen! What a CV!

"Millie, you are one in a million!" I said, in genuine awe. Just wow!

As I steeled myself to step into the unknown (i.e. through the door), my thoughts turned to the potential dangers that lurked beyond. I wasn't scared. I was desperate to carry on, but I needed to talk to Millie first. The last time she had put blind faith in me and joined me on a fact-finding mission, she had ended up being kidnapped by Derek Mooney and involved in a plane crash! Now we were about to follow him through a mysterious door!

"Millie, I really desperately want to find out what's going on behind this door, but if we do enter, we will potentially be putting ourselves in extreme danger. I can't make any false promises that everything will be ok. If you want to leave now then you need to let me know. After this point, there is no turning back."

My speech brought an unexpected response from Millie – laughter!

"You cannae go in there without me! You'll be haggis! We come as a team, and no way am I letting you have all the fun! Now, step aside – ladies first!"

Well it was good to know that the small matter of surviving a plane crash had not dampened her *joie de vivre*! She was right though – two heads were better than one, and in this crime-fighting duo, Millie was most certainly the yin to my yang!

"Of course. Ladies first! Where are my manners?" I said, smiling as I opened the door for her. I entered after her, closing the door behind me. We were in!

Turning on the torch on my camera phone, we took a look around. We were in quite a narrow passage, with wires and pipework exposed on the walls. As we wandered a little further in, we came to a stairwell and a sign that read 'NO UNAUTHORISED ACCESS BEYOND THIS POINT'.

"What do you think?" Millie asked. "Should we carry on?"

"Well, if we weren't deterred by a locked door that required an access code, then I don't see that a sign should cause us too much concern!" I replied.

"Fair point!" Millie half-whispered, responding with a smile.

We sidestepped the sign and started to walk down the stairs. Conscious of making too much noise, we tiptoed our way further and further down, the steel of the steps clanging gently as we went.

"How far beneath the surface of London must we be now?" Millie whispered.

"I'm not sure, but it feels like we are heading to the centre of the earth!" I replied.

Eventually we came to the very bottom of the stairwell and another door. This door had a bar across to open it, similar to one that you would find on any emergency exit. Tentatively, I eased the door open, and awaiting us was the most surprising sight!

We were standing on another platform, almost identical in every way to the one we had been stood on a few moments earlier. The only real differences were that there was no advertising to be seen, or any signs that informed you which station you were at. Oh, and this platform was completely deserted. How bizarre! At the far end of the platform, we could see a door being pulled shut with a loud slam.

"This is really weird! What on earth is this place? It's like a wee secret platform!" Millie exclaimed.

"I think that's exactly what it is! It clearly isn't being used. Well, for a start there are no people, but also no advertising or signs. Why would there be a secret platform though? It doesn't make any sense!" I pondered.

"I think I've given up on things making sense!" Millie stated. "It happened at roughly the moment that I met you!"

I guessed that was a compliment of sorts. In any case, this was no time to dwell! We had to decide what to do next…

"Ok Millie – a couple of questions. Do you think that it was Mooney that just disappeared into that door? Also, do you think he saw us?" I asked.

"I think it must have been him," Millie responded. "And he definitely didn't see us because I'm sure he'd have come back for us if he had!"

I thought on Millie's point for a moment. She was definitely right. He seemed so determined to exact his revenge on us, that he would not have been able to resist that golden opportunity.

"Yes, I think you're right," I agreed. "What do we do now though?"

"We've come this far. We need to at least see what is behind the door," Millie stated.

A few hours ago, Millie wanted us to leave London as soon as possible in case Derek Mooney tried to find us. Now, having been attacked and chased by Mooney, she was more than willing to enter a door that she already knew he was behind! It was all so illogical, but Millie had engaged detective-mode. And I liked it!

We wandered up to the door in question. It was almost identical to the one on the other platform, complete with combination lock. It couldn't be the same code could it?

"Try and enter the same code again Millie," I directed. Millie did so, but the door would not budge.

"I'm going to try it in reverse," Millie explained, tapping in the five-digit combination – 60810. She tried the handle again and the door opened.

"Amazing!" I remarked gleefully. "This has all been so easy! Well done!"

"Nae bother!" replied Millie with a smile. "She shoots, she scores!"

Our confident exuberance had come too early though. As we carefully entered the door, closing it quietly behind us, things were about to get an awful lot trickier...

# CHAPTER 10

We were now in a narrow corridor. The corridor was dimly lit, but it was possible to discern our surroundings. There was just one door, at the far end of the corridor, so our destination was somewhat predetermined. We wandered up to the door – this time there was no lock of any kind, just a regular handle. I eased the door open and we came to another narrow stairwell. By now we were beginning to become disorientated by all the different doors and stairs. I was not entirely sure that if required to, I would be able to find my way back to the platform we had left behind!

Just then we heard a voice. Then another voice. Gradually the conversation became louder and louder, as presumably the owners of the deep masculine voices got closer and closer.

"What do we do?" Millie whispered, suddenly sounding much more anxious. "Should we make a run for it?"

I tried the handle of the door we had originally entered through. It was wedged shut! I tried to prise it open, but to no avail. We were trapped!

"Right, think Peter, think!" I muttered to myself. "The voices seem to be coming from below. Let's go up these steps. Quickly Millie, run!"

We sprinted up the narrow stairwell in single file, with Millie ahead and me following just behind. At the top of the stairs was a small half-size door. Millie opened the door and we clambered in on all fours. After crawling inside this dark, narrow space I softly closed the door behind us.

"What is it about us and being trapped underground in confined spaces?" Millie whispered.

"Yes, it's a habit we probably need to shake," I replied.

We sat in silence for a few minutes. At this moment it occurred to me that we had not sent our parents one message since we said our goodbyes at Canada Water Station. There wasn't any hope of doing that now, with no phone signal this far underground. They had probably already phoned the police to report us missing, which right now could only be a good thing – not that the police would ever find us in our underground prison.

Suddenly and without warning, we were no longer sat in complete darkness. Millie and I could see each other clearly. Where was the light coming from? I looked behind me at the door that we had entered through. No, that was still closed.

"Look Peter, the light is coming from further in!" Millie whispered.

We scuttled along the tiny tunnel like hamsters following a trail of seeds. After ten or so metres, we came to the source of the light. The bright light was beaming through a large iron grate. We shuffled up to the grate and peered through. By this stage, given the events of the past year, I felt that generally very little could come as a shock to me any more – yet somehow, I was completely taken aback by the sight that greeted us.

Below us was a large conference room. Similar to one that you might find in a plush office building. A lawyers or architects offices perhaps. Not something you would expect to find hundreds of feet below one of the busiest parts of London. The room was well lit and stunningly decorated in marble effect, almost like a room in a Venetian Palazzo, with a huge mahogany conference table as the centrepiece. On the far wall of the room was a large screen, presumably for use with the projector that was fixed to the ceiling, not a million miles from the grate we were staring through. On the walls to the left and right were large corporate logos. The logo was of a golden wild animal – a big cat of some kind – with some writing underneath. Unfortunately, the writing was in Russian, a language which I have to admit, I wasn't fluent in.

"This is surreal!" Millie whispered.

"Very strange," I replied in an equally hushed tone. "What animal do you think that is, and what do you think it means?"

"It could be a lion, or a leopard maybe?" Millie offered. "As to what it means, who knows? One thing I do know is that this isn't right, is it? I'm getting the same feeling about this as I did when we discovered all those illegal medicines on Orsk."

"Yes, I strongly suspect that Mooney has led us straight to the secret headquarters of whatever organisation it is that he works for," I suggested. "If we weren't trapped with no obvious route of escape, we could congratulate ourselves on a job well done! As it is though, we're a little snookered."

As I uttered these words, the seats around the conference table slowly started to fill as a range of different people flooded into the room.

"Peter, it looks like a meeting is about to happen. Quick, you have to record it on your phone!" suggested Millie.

"Great idea Mildred," I replied, grabbing my phone from my pocket and holding it up ready to record.

There must have been around twenty people now seated around the huge table, and the accompanying sound of a gentle murmur of muted conversation. I squinted to try and see some of the faces. I instantly recognised the slicked black hair and stumpy figure of Derek Mooney, still looking as angry as he was when he kicked the wall. He was sitting snarling and muttering to himself, not partaking in the conversational pleasantries around the table.

Suddenly, the room was silenced by the entrance of a suited gentleman, who took his place at the head of the conference table. The man looked about sixty years old, and had short grey hair and a short, neatly-groomed grey beard. He was wearing dark glasses and a black suit, which looked extremely expensive and was tailored to perfection. He had the look of someone that although slightly advanced in years, kept himself extremely fit. He was flanked on either side by giant identical twins, both of whom were also wearing suits. They must have been about seven feet tall and almost as broad! I deduced that they were likely security guards for the grey-haired gentleman.

The gentlemen took his seat as the two henchmen stayed standing to attention behind him. The man removed his glasses to reveal piercing blue eyes, that even from the distance we were at, looked like they could cut through diamonds.

"Good afternoon ladies and gentleman, or should I say 'privet'?" the man said, in a thick Russian accent but with perfectly fluent English. The group sat around the table laughed politely but mutedly, as if afraid of what would happen if they did not. "To any newcomers around the table, welcome to the UK headquarters of Zolotaya Pantera. We do, of course, have a base in almost every major world capital but there is something particularly special about this place, deep below the wonderful city of London."

The rest of the group around the table were deathly silent. My best description of the atmosphere was somewhere between expectant and terrified. It was fascinating to watch this gentleman speak, his eyes shifting slowly around everyone at the table, as if to check their complete focus remained steadfastly on him.

"For anyone that hasn't met me before, my name is Aleksandr Zolotov. I am the founder and co-owner of Zolotaya Pantera, or to translate for our English colleagues and guests, 'Golden Panther'. Zolotaya Pantera is a multinational organisation that turns over billions of euros per year. Some of this through entirely legitimate means! However, I think you know that's not why you are here today!" the man continued. This last comment, sneered rather than spoken, was met by a roar of laughter from the table.

"He must be the 'big boss' of the criminal gang," I whispered to Millie.

"I dinnae like him! Not one bit!" Millie replied. I had to agree – he seemed a pretty scary character.

Zolotov continued. "Now, before we get down to business, I want to introduce you to our two esteemed guests. We are lucky to have them working with us. They are here to ensure that everything goes to plan, with no slip ups. Thank you for joining us…Dame Harriet Rodwell and the right honourable Henry Mawden-Smythe MP."

My jaw almost dropped to the floor in shock.

# CHAPTER 11

Dame Harriet Rodwell and Henry Mawden-Smythe MP were two personalities that I knew an awful lot about, as they regularly featured in my dad's daily newspaper. Dad always buys one of those massive newspapers that is impossible to hold and read at the same time. It's so annoying! I usually just take the sport section to read, but occasionally I catch up on some of the news as well. Anyway, I digress slightly – my point is that these two characters were very important and influential people.

Dame Harriet Rodwell was the Commissioner of the Metropolitan Police. In other words, the most senior police officer in the country, and the person in charge of London's police force. She had the reputation as being a really tough, uncompromising character. 'Tough on crime, tough on criminals' was her catchy motto. Her reputation was absolutely impeccable so why would she be getting involved in all of this? It seemed very strange - surely she earned enough money to be more than comfortable in her impending retirement?

Henry Mawden-Smythe MP was an entirely different matter altogether. I was not remotely surprised to see him involved in underground activity (in this case literally). He had a reputation for being right at the centre of all sorts of different political scandals – cash for questions, claiming fraudulent expenses, bribery – you name it, he had probably been involved in it. He was a man of huge ambition but sadly very little talent and even fewer morals. Inexplicably, after a career of being a fairly low-key 'back bench' Member of Parliament, he currently held one of the most important jobs in the country as Home Secretary. I'm sure it's entirely coincidental, but the newly elected Prime Minister happened to be his cousin. Make of that what you will!

Mawden-Smythe spoke up. "Thank you, Mr Zolotov. I'm sure I speak for my good friend and colleague Harriet when I say we're delighted to be here. Please feel free to go about your business as you normally would. Think of us as an insurance policy. If everything goes to plan tonight, which I'm sure it will, then we will remain very much in the background. Then after the event, we will help to ensure that everything gets brushed under the carpet, as it were."

"Did you hear that Millie?" I whispered. "Tonight! They are planning something tonight!"

"Oh, dearie me! Who are the man and lady that were just introduced? They sounded important," Millie replied.

"You could say that!" I said. "Whatever is being planned is on such a large scale that these Golden Panther people obviously feel that they need some high-level officials on board to try and cover it up afterwards. It also means that we have to be very careful who we go to with any information – if we make it out of here that is!"

"Thank you, Henry – you are a good man," Zolotov said, awarding Mawden-Smythe with a pat on the shoulder, very much in the same way a dog owner would praise his prize pooch. "Now, one more run-through of tonight's plan. You should all know your roles by now. Mistakes will not be tolerated."

With that, Zolotov turned on the projector by pressing a button on his mobile phone. The projector displayed an image of what appeared to be a map of Trafalgar Square, alongside a cross-section diagram of both above and below ground.

"Ok, I will go through this quickly. Listen carefully, there will be no interruptions and no questions. Understand? Good. As you know, for several months Dmitri, one of our very best men, has been working at the National Gallery as a security guard. Getting to know the whole place inside out – all of the systems, the best ways in and out, the location of all of the works of art – everything. At exactly 12:30am, Dmitri will shut off the gallery's CCTV. Immediately afterwards, he will disable all security and back-up security systems and alarms. By this time, all of the areas of the gallery will be unguarded as Dmitri will have earlier laced the drinks of the other security guards with a strong tranquiliser. Thus, the scene is set for the greatest Art heist of all time."

Zolotov said this with such relish, in the way you would hope a master-villain to deliver his grand plan.

"What a brilliant plan! Just a question though – how do we get the paintings out of the gallery without being seen?" Derek Mooney interjected.

"SILENCE! How dare you interrupt me when I'm taking a dramatic pause? Do not interrupt me again Mooney! Who do you think you are?" Zolotov screamed in response.

"Sorry boss," whimpered a terrified looking Mooney.

"Anyway, as I was about to say – the next part of the plan is the real masterstroke. You will have noticed the large diagram. This diagram shows the National Gallery – both above and below ground. Below the gallery is a secret tunnel." Zolotov pointed to the map, specifically the location of this tunnel.

"That is genius!" I quietly remarked to Millie. "Can you see? That tunnel leads all the way down to the secret platform!"

"When Dmitri has seen off the security guards, he will open up the doors at the entrance to the tunnel and at this point the rest of you will enter. In pairs you will proceed straight to your allocated painting, remove it from the wall and bring it straight back down the tunnel and to the platform. The train will be waiting at the platform to load the paintings onto. The train will leave at exactly 1:30am. It must not be a second late, as this will comprise the journey and clear passage of the train. You should all know your jobs by now. Is that all clear?" Zolotov concluded.

"Yes!" shouted almost all of those seated around the table, pretty much in unison. Derek Mooney tentatively lifted his hand, like he was in a classroom and Zolotov was his rather intimidating teacher.

"Ah, Mr Mooney. How terribly forgetful of me. I forgot that you had not been here, so this will be the first time you have heard the plan. Did you have a question?" Zolotov asked menacingly.

"Thanks Boss. Yeah, I just wondered what I would be doing? What's my role?" Mooney asked.

"What's your role? What's your role? Let me see…" Zolotov contemplated, whilst scratching his beard. "Ladies and gentlemen. If you haven't met him yet, this is Derek Mooney. Mr Mooney was our head of operations up in Scotland, but that didn't go too well for you did it?"

Mooney was visibly shaken. He didn't like the way this was going.

"I suppose not," Mooney muttered.

"I suppose not!" echoed Zolotov, mimicking Mooney's cockney accent. "Well let's see. Were you outsmarted by a couple of teenagers? Yes, you were! Did you waste years of careful planning and one of our best routes to smuggle goods into the UK? Yes, you did! Did your sloppiness cost us millions of euros in lost revenue? Yes, it did! Did we have to break you out of prison at great risk and expense to the organisation? Yes, we did! Basically, you owe me! You also owe many of these good people! This cannot go unpunished!"

Zolotov was gradually getting angrier and angrier, and

more and more animated, spitting with every single syllable. Millie and I watched on in horror as Zolotov's two huge bodyguards walked around the table and positioned themselves directly behind Mooney. One of them pushed him onto the table and held him down. The other twin grabbed Mooney's left arm, pushed it down against the table and with a single movement grabbed a knife from his pocket and sliced off Mooney's little finger!

"AAAAARRRRRGGGGGHHHHH!" Mooney screamed in agony. Millie closed her eyes. My heart was bouncing up and down. I was horrified and amazed by how easily the finger came off.

"That was fun!" Zolotov exclaimed, with a disturbed look in his eyes. "You see Mr Mooney. You still owe me. You've caused me to lose far more than a single digit! Let's call this one a down payment. Any more mistakes and the price will be considerably greater!"

Zolotov then turned to address the rest of the table. "I'm sorry you had to see that ladies and gentlemen. Unfortunately, mistakes are not tolerated by Zolotaya Pantera! This should be a warning to everyone! Perfection is demanded!"

At that moment Millie grabbed my arm tightly. I looked at her face, which was contorted into the most unusual shape. She closed her eyes. Oh no, not now! Was she going to...

"AAAACCCCHHHHHOOOOOOOOOOOOOO!"

Millie led out the almightiest sneeze. Everyone sat around the table immediately looked up to see where the sound was coming from.

"Well, it appears we have uninvited guests! How rude! Nikolai, Nikifor – find whoever this is and bring them to me!" ordered Zolotov.

Millie and I looked at each other and in unison we shouted "RUN!"

# CHAPTER 12

Without sufficient space to turn around in our dark, narrow corridor of uncertainty, Millie and I shuffled backwards as quickly as we possibly could. It was uncomfortable, ungainly and ultimately in vain. Waiting for us at the door were Zolotov's huge bodyguards Nikolai and Nikifor. I fancied that we could comfortably outrun them but unfortunately for us, they were able to grab us as we opened the door.

As much as we both struggled and squirmed, the vice-like grip of the two colossal men was far too strong for us to prise ourselves out of. We were carried down the stairs like we were rag dolls, each man with one of us under their arm. Though carried along sideways, I noticed that we passed the door we had originally entered through but been unable to prise open to escape. We kept going down another flight of stairs, along a tight, oppressive corridor and through another door into a small, stuffy room with no windows. I was thrown with no little force down to the ground. Fortunately, I was able to push my arms out in front of me to break my fall somewhat, but it was still a painful landing. I barely had time to catch my breath before Millie came hurtling towards me. I was able to half-catch her to prevent any injury, but nonetheless it must have been an equally uncomfortable landing. As we lay there in an aching mess on the floor, one of the men grabbed my mobile phone from my pocket and threw it against the wall. I watched it smash into a million pieces. My brand-new phone was gone, and along with it any evidence of the meeting in the conference room.

The two muscle-bound giants took their places on wooden chairs by either side of the door. This was obviously a tried and tested routine. There they sat and stared at us. Minutes turned into hours; the silence only broken by the occasional distant rumble of a train. Every so often I tried to look at Millie but whenever I did, the men would hiss, as if to warn that any communication, verbal or non-verbal, would not be looked upon favourably. From my position seated on the rock-hard floor, I looked around at the room instead. It was a very small room, about the size my bedroom at home, with no distinguishing features whatsoever. The floor, walls and ceiling were a murky grey concrete. What was concerning were several small holes in the walls, which looked very much like bullet holes.

For the first time since our chase through the London Underground had begun, I had some time to think and reflect. Yesterday I was meeting the Queen as a national hero. This morning I was competing in an Athletics final in front of a massive crowd. Now I was in a small concrete box several metres underneath the hustle and bustle of London, with no likely prospect of escape. I thought about my family and how worried they would be right now. I thought about Millie's parents and all that they had already been through, with Millie's accident and Mr McCluskey being held prisoner by the same evil gang we were now at the mercy of. I thought about my dear friend Finny whose life was cut tragically short, and his father Captain Finn, who was now consigned to a wheelchair for the rest of his life. All of this because of this gang – Zolotaya Pantera – and their wicked pursuits.

One thing was for certain. If I did by some twist of fate manage to make it out of here alive, I was going to make it my life's work to bring down Zolotaya Pantera and expose Aleksandr Zolotov and his cronies to the world. I had to – for Finny, for Captain Finn, for Mr McCluskey, for Millie, and for every other person whose lives had been impacted by this cash-rich but morally bankrupt organisation.

My deep thoughts were broken by the abrupt creaking sound of the door being opened. Appearing as if an angel of darkness was the man himself – Aleksandr Zolotov!

"Hello! Welcome to our home! I hope you like what we've done with the place?" Zolotov quipped, rather pleased with his own joke. "You must be the famous Peter and Millie? I've heard so much about you!"

Millie and I looked back at him in silence for a moment. Inside I felt a strange mix of fear and rage. I hated this man. My best friend was dead because of him. I had everything to say to him but yet nothing to say to him. Luckily Millie broke the silence for me.

"Well, I've never heard of you!"

"Ha ha! Well, that's as it should be – any criminal mastermind that is well known to the public is probably behind bars!" Zolotov retorted, seeming to enjoy Millie's comeback. "You are a feisty madam, aren't you? It's the red hair – my mama always said that anyone with red hair has more than a little of the devil in them. So, me and you are not so different after all."

"Was your mother an evil murderer too?" I blurted, much to even my own surprise.

"Well, the skinny boy speaks. You are a spirited pair, aren't you?" Zolotov said. With that he wandered towards me and grabbed my face hard with his hand whilst looking me dead in the eye. "Though I should warn you, if you mention my mama's name in vain one more time, it will be the last thing you ever say."

Relinquishing his grasp, Zolotov took a couple of steps back. I caught my breath and looked at Millie. This man was very bad news indeed.

Zolotov continued. "Actually, I have to say I am very impressed. Very impressed indeed. You two are clearly a few steps ahead of Mooney, that is for certain. First you somehow bring down our whole Scotland operation, which cost me an awful lot of money by the way. Then you manage to locate our London headquarters and find out a great number of things that you should not know about. Quite brilliant really!"

This was somewhat unexpected. Why was he suddenly complimenting us? Was this some kind of reverse psychology or a tactic to catch us off guard? Either way, it was puzzling.

"By the way, did you like my plan? I'm curious to know what you clever little junior spies make of it?" Zolotov asked. He folded his arms and walked from side to side, pacing across the room but maintaining eye contact at all times. "You may have wondered how I persuaded two such prominent public figures to get involved? Hmmm?"

I sensed that Zolotov wanted us to play his game. The situation that we found ourselves in was not the best position for bargaining. At this point my feeling was that it was probably better to reply than not. I needed to play smart. I needed to play to Zolotov's sizable ego. I decided to put my anger to the back of my mind, if only temporarily. I have to admit I was also more than a tiny bit intrigued to find out.

"How did you manage to get them involved?" I asked calmly and with a hint of eagerness in my voice. "I really would like to know."

Millie looked at me quizzically.

"Would you now?" responded Zolotov, clearly delighted that I was playing along. "Well, as you might imagine, getting Mawden-Smythe on board was as easy as taking Pryaniki from a baby. That man would do pretty much anything for a sack full of cash! That's politicians for you! Dame Harriet was a little trickier – until I kidnapped her husband that is! Now I say 'jump' and she say 'how high!' Ha ha!"

"You're a bad man!" shouted Millie, unable to control her rage any longer. She moved forward as if to lunge at him, but I held her back with all my might.

"Thank you," laughed Zolotov, apparently completed unperturbed by this. "Don't worry. When this is over, she can have her husband back. I've just not decided in how many pieces yet! Ha ha!"

Millie was almost hyperventilating next to me; her breathing was that heavy. I needed to change the subject, and quickly.

"One thing I don't quite understand about all this is why are you stealing all these famous paintings? Surely as soon as you try to sell them, people will know they are stolen and will report you?"

"Good question young man! Top of the class!" Zolotov replied, seeming genuinely impressed. "You are of course correct. However, these paintings are not going to be sold on. They are being delivered to some of the richest men on the planet. Billionaires who've made their money in the oil and gas industries. They have everything they've ever wanted, but we can get them things that money can't buy. Imagine having a Cezanne, a Van Gogh, a Titian in your private collection. Paintings that people travel half way around the planet to see are now for your eyes only. That's what these men want, and we are going to deliver them gift-wrapped, for a healthy price of course."

That sounded like the very definition of greed to me. Taking something beautiful that can be enjoyed by millions of people every year, and hiding it away for your eyes only. I nodded as if I understood but really nothing could be further from my way of thinking. Just remember, play the game…

"Listen. Peter, Millie. I have to go now, but before I do, I'm going to make you a one-time offer. Come and work for me!" Zolotov uttered to our total amazement.

"Zolotaya Pantera could do with two intelligent and athletic young people like yourselves. We have a training programme for new recruits, not that you need it, but I think you two could be incredible. You would earn money beyond your wildest dreams. Travel the world. See everywhere you've ever wanted to see. What do you say?"

Before I'd even had time to process these unexpected words, Millie had an answer for him.

"No thank you Mr Zolotov. We've seen the way you treat employees, and I'm actually very attached to my fingers!"

Zolotov laughed heartily. Looking around to his mountainous bodyguards he shouted, "Attached! I love it! Ha ha! She's funny! You're funny!" With that he turned and walked towards the door. The two burly men opened the door for Zolotov, but before walking through he turned around to have the final word.

"Very well. Have it your way. I thought you might want to do things the easy way, but no matter. You *will* work for me, but it will be as my prisoners! My slaves! I'm sure I'll find a use for you both. Now if you don't mind, I have work to do." With that Zolotov vanished to enact his latest evil plan.

# CHAPTER 13

With Zolotov having left the room, we were once again alone with the two silent giants. I had not yet resigned myself to a life of slavery, but things looked increasingly bleak. It felt like we had been in that room for hour upon hour, but in reality, I had no idea what the time was – my phone was smashed and my watch had stopped working when I was thrown to the ground earlier.

I had been trying to concoct an escape plan in my head, but I was struggling. Everything I could think of involved a huge level of risk. I felt that it was now or never though. If we did not get away tonight, when we vaguely knew where we were, what chance did we have if we were taken to a new and strange location, most likely blindfolded? I sneakily glanced at Millie out of the corner of my eye, just in time to see a single tear splash from her eye onto the concrete floor. I needed to find a way out. I owed it to her.

I thought of a vague sketch of a plan. It was most likely a terrible idea that could backfire in the worst possible way, however at this stage there seemed little to lose.

I gestured as if I was getting a little uncomfortable and stretched slightly, making sure to put my hands behind my back. Just behind where I was sitting was a small wooden panel at the base of the wall. It may have been a piece of skirting board at one stage but rather than going all the way around the room it was probably only a metre or so long. I waited for a few minutes until the two men seemed slightly distracted and then with my right hand knocked hard on the wood. The two men looked at each other and in unison stood up to open the door, assuming that their boss was back to have some more fun at the expense of his prisoners. Just as one of the men turned the handle, I quickly propelled myself into a crouching position and launched into a full-out sprint, as if Usain Bolt powering out of the blocks upon the sound of the starting pistol. In a flash I dived through the legs of one of the men and flung myself through the narrow door opening.

The two men must have caught sight of me at exactly the same moment as they both leant down to try and grab me. In the process their heads collided at an almighty velocity. The hideous crunching sound reverberated around the concrete cell at a volume that two colliding skulls should not make. I'm reluctant to use the phrase 'the bigger they come, the harder they fall' as it seems a little clichéd. However, it certainly befitted the occasion, as the two men were instantly knocked unconscious and slumped to the ground in a mangled heap of flesh. In particular the sound of one of the men hitting the deck face first will haunt me forever! It may not have been exactly what I intended, but through a little athleticism and a lot of luck, we had fresh hope of an escape.

"What have I just seen?" Millie gasped in disbelief at the black comedy of the situation.

"I thought I'd try a little something!" I replied with a sudden spring in my step.

"You could have gotten us both killed!" Millie said. She sounded half exasperated, half awestruck at the cavalier act that I had just pulled.

"Coulda woulda shoula!" came my smirking response. "Now come on, let's go. We need to be quick!"

Millie stood up and ran out of the room to join me in the corridor, giving me a large clout on the arm to both congratulate and admonish me for my latest stunt. We made our way along the corridor and up the stairs completely unchallenged. We came to the door that had proved too stiff to open before. Both pushing down together on the handle and leaning our shoulders into the rusty door we managed to prise it open. Again, another deserted corridor! This was proving far too simple. One more door and then we would be back out onto the secret platform.

"Let me go first," I offered. "I'm sure there will be some of Zolotov's men on the platform. They may be armed."

"I'm nae sure it will make a great deal of difference. If there's a man with a gun on the other side of that door, we're toast anyway!" Millie pointed out. It was a fair point.

"Millie look, if we don't make it out into the daylight, I want you to know that you're a pretty incredible friend. I know it sounds a strange thing to say but our times together have been some of the best fun I've ever had, despite the odd near-death experience here and there!" I said with utmost sincerity.

Millie laughed, leaned over and kissed me on the forehead.

"That's for luck!" she said, smiling broadly. "Now let's get out of here!"

"Ok. When I give the signal, sprint like you've never sprinted before to the door we entered through," I directed. "Ready. Three, two, one, go!"

With that, we flung open the door and ran as fast as our legs could take us. There was nobody standing between us and the door. We just needed to get through that door, up the stairs and we were back with the general public again.

"You two! Again!" a voice shouted from behind us. I recognised it instantly as Derek Mooney. "You're not getting away this time!"

As we neared the door, the musty underground air filled with the piercing screech of a gun being fired. It felt as if the bullet almost brushed past my ear as it punched a hole in the door. I lunged for the door pulling the handle and ushering Millie through. I dived in behind her just as a second shot was fired, again missing me by millimetres as the bullet once again made its way through the poor defenceless door! I scrambled to my feet and we raced up the metal steps, clanging as we went. At the top we barged through the door and there we were! Back once again amongst the public. I had never been so pleased to see a crowded platform.

"Keep moving!" I breathlessly muttered to Millie. "Better to make sure we're away from here, just in case."

As we slowed down our run to a fast walking past to try and blend in with the crowd, I noticed that we were getting quite a lot of strange looks. We must have appeared somewhat dishevelled after the traumatic afternoon we had endured. There were holes in my jeans from where I'd been thrown to the ground by Zolotov's bodyguard and all our clothes were filthy from our scrambled escape.

We made our way up the escalator to the ticket barriers. It was at this point that I remembered that we had jumped the barriers at Waterloo Station during our original attempt to escape from Derek Mooney, so didn't actually have tickets.

"Erm, Millie. We don't actually have a ticket to get through the barriers," I stated.

"Ah! Do you have one of those wee mussel cards instead?" Millie asked.

"Millie! You're funny! It's an Oyster card!" I chuckled.

"I knew it was some type of seafood!" said Millie indignantly. "Anyway, do you have one?"

"No. I'm thirteen! I live in rural Cambridgeshire. I don't have an Oyster Card!" I retorted. "We'll have to just try and sneak through behind someone else quickly before the barrier closes."

As we got to the barrier, I noticed there was a lady checking that everyone had a ticket. Typical! Just our luck!

What else could go wrong? There was no point trying anything. We had to come clean!

"Excuse me," I said to the lady. "I'm afraid we don't have a ticket."

"We're really sorry," Millie added. "We've had a very strange day!"

The lady looked us up and down. She was quite a large lady, in height and width, and was wearing a sizable frown on her face. She didn't look impressed.

"Please let us through," said Millie, pleading our case. "We haven't got any money on us. We just want to go home! Please!"

All of a sudden, the lady's expression changed as if she'd had a lightbulb moment.

"Wait a minute! I know you!" she said to Millie.

"You do?" Millie said, sounding puzzled.

The lady took a phone out of her pocket and started typing. In a few seconds, she turned the screen to show us something. "Look!"

There it was. The video of Millie fainting in front of the Queen! Just this time it was set to music – 'Jam' by Michael Jackson! Somebody had edited the clip to show Millie collapsing and then reversing the video to show her getting to her feet again. This was repeated several times over. The lady was almost in tears of laughter by now.

"I can't believe I've just met the jam girl!" the lady said. "Can I get a selfie?"

"Does that mean you're going to let us through?" I asked, with a growing sense of urgency.

"It's a deal!" she replied. "Anyways, what happened to you to? You look dreadful!"

"It's a long story!" I replied.

After a quick photo op with this week's newest viral sensation, the lady sent us on our way. As we wandered out of Charing Cross Station, we were free! The fresh London air had never felt so good. It was a beautiful crisp, clear night. It felt a little chilly, as it often does when you're tired, but none of that mattered right now.

As we wandered across a relatively quiet Trafalgar Square, I gazed up at the sky. Even through the London smog there was no mistaking Finny's Star, resplendent as ever. Millie noticed me looking up and instantly knew what I was doing. She grabbed my hand and squeezed it gently. As I looked at her, she smiled softly, and we continued our walk arm-in-arm.

"So..." Millie said, pausing slightly. "What now?"

# CHAPTER 14

Having escaped from Zolotov and our underground prison, we decided our best option was to try and find Du'ane's apartment. With no phones or map this was not going to be as easy as it might have been. Luckily, I had memorised the address and we knew that the apartment was on Trafalgar Square, so we did at least have a reasonable chance. We wandered from building to building looking at the numbers next to the doors until I found what I thought might be the right one.

"I think it could be this one," I said.

"Well, we may as well give it a go," Millie replied. "Though if we're wrong, be prepared for some angry folk being woken up late on a Sunday night!"

I pressed on the buzzer and we waited for a minute or so. Nothing. Undeterred, I buzzed another time. Again, we waited. Eventually we heard a deep, slightly bleary male voice on the intercom.

"Yes, who is this? It's nearly midnight and I have work in the morning," the voice mumbled, sounding extremely grumpy.

"Mr Joseph? Is that you? It's Peter Lipscombe, Du'ane's friend," I replied.

The tone of the man's voice changed instantly. "Peter? Thank goodness! Your parents have reported you as a missing person. They are so worried. You'd better get inside!"

With that, we heard a buzzing sound and Millie pushed open the door. We entered the building and started to climb up the rather posh looking marble staircase. We kept going up the seemingly endless staircase, past floor after floor until we got to the fifth floor. On the landing Mr Joseph was waiting for us. Mr Joseph was a tall and imposing man, but also a gentle sort and one of the cleverest people you could hope to meet. He was usually to be found in his trademark grey suit, large black-rimmed spectacles and one of a range of brightly coloured ties, hinting at his Carribean roots following a childhood spent in Antigua. However, on this occasion he was wearing a black and red silk kimono-style dressing gown. It was quite a fashion statement!

"What on earth has happened to you two?" Mr Joseph asked, having noticed our bedraggled appearance and tatty clothes. "My wife is on the phone to your parents letting them know you are ok. They all got back to Cambridge, but are now on their way back to London after you didn't turn up here. You'd better come inside."

The apartment was exactly as Du'ane had described to us earlier. It was a large open-plan space, with a kitchen and dining area, a seating area with the biggest television I'd ever seen and at the far end a pool table. I wandered past the window and took in the magnificent view of Trafalgar Square. We were directly opposite the National Gallery, where in about half an hour Zolotov and his men would be helping themselves to some of the most magnificent paintings ever committed to canvas.

Mrs Joseph was seated on the sofa, wearing an identical dressing gown to Mr Joseph. 'His and hers' dressing gowns were not a sight that I was prepared for! I'm not sure, given the day that we'd had, that it was the most shocking thing that we'd seen today, but it was certainly high up the list! Mrs Joseph was on the telephone speaking to my mum. Even though it wasn't on speakerphone, I could hear my mum's voice crystal clear. She only has one volume, bless her!

"Peter, can you speak to your mum please?" Mrs Joseph asked, before passing the phone to me.

"Hi Mum. Are you alright?" I asked.

"No Peter, I'm not great! We've been worried sick. Neither you or Millie have answered your phones all day. We've left hundreds of messages. What happened?" Mum said. She sounded close to tears.

"Sorry Mum. It's a long story. We haven't got our phones I'm afraid, so didn't receive your messages," I replied.

"At least you're safe and well. That's the main thing. Is Millie there with you?" asked Mum, calming down slightly.

"Yes, Millie's here and she's fine as well. Sorry for spoiling your day. Say sorry to the McCluskeys for me as well," I added.

"I will do Peter. Look, we're on the train back to London at the moment. Go and get some sleep now, but me and your dad will want a proper explanation from you in the morning," said Mum. Oh dear, that usually meant I was in big trouble. "Can you put Millie on now please, her mum would like a word?"

I passed the phone to Millie. She spoke to her parents for a few minutes before passing the phone back to Mrs Joseph. Neither of us had mentioned anything about the business with Derek Mooney, Aleksandr Zolotov and his henchmen. It didn't seem like the right time. That didn't mean we'd given up on foiling Zolotov's master plan though!

Whilst we'd been on the phone to our parents, Du'ane had made his way through from his room. He had gone to the effort of throwing on a T-shirt and jeans, though I suspected that was more for Millie's benefit than mine.

"Guys, what has gone on tonight?" Du'ane asked. "Everyone has been panicking. You should have been here hours ago."

"Yes, we're really glad you're both ok, but I think we

are owed an explanation," chipped in Mr Joseph.

Taking a deep breath, I began to tell the stunned Joseph family everything that had happened since we left our parents at Canada Water Station that morning. Millie being grabbed by Mooney. Being chased by Mooney through the underground. The secret platform. Discovering Zolotaya Pantera's hidden London headquarters. Finding out about the plot to raid the National Gallery. Being discovered and imprisoned. Finally, escaping and making our way to the apartment. Quite an afternoon!

"Now we need to find a way to stop them," I explained. "Stop them from stealing the paintings and ensure they are bought to justice. Zolotov, Mooney and the rest of them."

"We need to call the police," said Mr Joseph authoritatively.

"We can't, Mr Joseph," I replied. "Zolotov has the head of the Metropolitan Police working for him. If we contact the police about something this serious, she will be alerted immediately and it will be dismissed as a hoax. We'll probably also have some of Zolotov's henchmen sent to find us before we cause any more trouble."

"Woah, this is heavy!" Du'ane added unhelpfully.

"We need to do something, and quickly," added Millie. "Very soon they will be breaking in and starting to remove the paintings. Any ideas?"

"Well…" said Mr Joseph, "usually when people feel they won't be listened to by those in positions of authority, they would go to the media."

"Mr Joseph, you work for the BBC," I said. "Could you tell them all about this, and perhaps they could do a story on the news and then it can't be ignored can it?"

"Do you have any proof?" asked Mr Joseph. "Otherwise the news team couldn't run the story."

I thought about the video that I'd filmed on my smartphone, that was lying smashed to pieces somewhere underneath London. That would have been as damning evidence as you could hope for. My heart sank.

"No, unfortunately not," I replied, with more than a note of resignation in my voice.

Just then, I had a faint outline of an idea.

"What if…" I pondered. "We did something that was so big, so unexpected, that it couldn't be ignored?"

"Now I like the sound of this!" Du'ane said, becoming more animated.

"What are you thinking Peter?" asked Millie.

I thought for a moment or two longer. It was a long shot, but I thought I may as well ask.

"Mr Joseph, Du'ane mentioned that you worked on the BBC election programme?" I said. My dad had forced me to watch the first few hours of the previous year's general election coverage as part of my 'ongoing political education'.

"I did," Mr Joseph confirmed.

"Did you have anything to do with the bits where the election results were projected onto the side of buildings?" I continued.

"Yes, it was my team that worked on the graphics for that," said Mr Joseph. "I actually have one of the more powerful projectors that we use here in the apartment, ready for a project we're working on tomorrow."

My eyes suddenly lit up. The sketch of an idea had rapidly become a fully formed oil painting befitting of a grand master.

"I've got it guys. Listen very carefully. Here's the plan…"

# CHAPTER 15

I had the bit between my teeth now and a determination to stop Zolotov in his tracks. The time was now 12:30am. Zolotov's men would be starting to enter the National Gallery. We had to work quickly.

"Mr Joseph, could I borrow your laptop and projector please?" I asked.

"No Peter, you can't borrow them," Mr Joseph replied solemnly. My heart sank. My plan was a non-starter. I was beyond disappointed. What now?

"You can't borrow them," Mr Joseph continued, "because we're all going to work together. What's the plan? What do you need?"

Yes! I loved Mr Joseph at that moment! What a guy!

"Right here's the plan," I began. "We're going to project the world's biggest PowerPoint presentation onto the front of the National Gallery! It's going to be completely impossible to ignore. We can then film it on a mobile phone and send in the footage to all the news channels. What do you think?"

"Sounds like a wicked plan!" Du'ane shouted eagerly. "Can I help?"

"Of course. It's going to be a team effort," I replied. "Mr Joseph, you're the expert. What do you think?"

"I think it could work. I'll go and put the projector on charge now," Mr Joseph replied. "There is also a lightweight camera somewhere in the apartment. I could film it on that."

"Even better!" I exclaimed.

I began work on my PowerPoint presentation. It had to be bold. It had to be colourful. It had to say everything that I needed it to say, but in as few words as possible. Most of all, we had to work quickly. Du'ane and Millie crowded around the laptop, offering up suggestions. Mr and Mrs Joseph ran off to find all the equipment that we needed, and thankfully to change out of their kimonos into something a little more suitable!

"I still can't believe you guys," commented Du'ane as we worked. "You're just so brave! You've just escaped from being imprisoned by a criminal gang, and your first thought is to put yourselves potentially back in harms way to try and stop them! It's crazy – you're like secret agents or something!"

This meant a lot from Du'ane. I admired him so much, not just for his athletic ability but also for being an all-round great guy. Now was not the time to get side-tracked though. I got my head down and ploughed on. Whilst beavering away, we could all hear Mr Joseph speaking to someone on the telephone. After speaking for a few minutes, Mr and Mrs Joseph re-entered the living area with two large cases, presumably the projector and the camera. Mr Joseph was now dressed in his trademark grey suit, whilst Mrs Joseph was somewhat more casual, wearing a colourful stripy woollen garment that was too long to be a jumper but too short to be a skirt, and deep purple leggings. Her blonde hair had been thrown into a pony tail and perched on the end of her nose, in contrast to the monster frames sported by Mr Joseph, were the tiniest pair of gold-rimmed glasses you had ever seen. Two distinctive looks!

"Right everyone. I have some good news," said Mr Joseph. "I have just been speaking to one of my colleagues at the BBC News Channel. They have said that it has been a really slow news day, and if we can set this up and get everything to work properly, they will run a live feed of our slideshow as breaking news!"

"That's incredible!" replied Millie triumphantly. "Does that mean they believe us?"

"My colleague was a little sceptical," Mr Joseph replied. "However, from her perspective, either way it's news! Either it's true and they have a major exclusive, or it's not and they have some crazy people projecting some outlandish allegations onto a famous London building, which isn't exactly something that happens every day! Also...I..."

Mr Joseph suddenly slowed his speech down and stopped himself mid-sentence as if he was about to admit something that he would rather not.

"What did you do Dad?" Du'ane asked bluntly, in a way that Millie or I would not have done.

"Sorry Millie!" Mr Joseph said. "I told her that the story involved the girl who fainted in front of the Queen! If it's any consolation, that's what seemed to swing it!"

We all laughed including Millie. It seems that a news story about attempting to catch an international crime syndicate in the act, whilst they perform the biggest art heist in history is of secondary importance to finding out the latest movements of someone who collapsed in front of the Queen!

"How are you getting on with your presentation?" Mrs Joseph asked, in a non-too subtle attempt to move the conversation on.

"I think we're done!" I said. "It'll have to do anyway. We need to get going, it's coming up to 1am!"

With that, we grabbed everything we needed and made our way to the door.

"Quick, throw these on!" shouted Du'ane, launching two of his designer sweatshirts in the direction of Millie and I. "You can't go out in public looking like that!"

We threw on the sweatshirts over our tatty, ripped clothing and made our way down the marble staircase and out into the London night air once more. I carried Mr Joseph's laptop in hand, with Du'ane and Millie walking either side of me. Mr and Mrs Joseph were a few paces behind, carrying the bags containing the projector and camera respectively.

"I'm just going to find the best place to set up the projector," Mr Joseph informed us, before proceeding to direct us. He was in work mode now! "Annabel, can you set up the camera onto its tripod please? You'll need to be just slightly to one side of where I am. Peter and Millie, I think you should be in front of the camera narrating the slides as they appear. It'll be a much more powerful piece of television if you are able to tell everyone about what the slides mean and your experiences. Du'ane, can you find the microphone that is in the bag with the camera? Please plug that into the camera and then kneel down slightly out of shot and hold it up towards Peter and Millie so that the sound quality will be really clear."

"Are you kidding me?" protested Du'ane. "I'm the sound guy? Behind the scenes? Does this face not scream front of camera to you?"

We all creased up laughing. I wasn't totally sure that he was joking, which in some ways made it even funnier!

"Yes dear, you're absolutely beautiful!" said Mrs Joseph, smiling gently. "Now run along and get that microphone! We've got a broadcast to set up!"

Whilst Mr and Mrs Joseph spent a couple of minutes setting up their equipment, ably assisted by Du'ane, the 'sound guy', I had the opportunity to check in with Millie, who was beginning to look a little bit nervous.

"Are you ok Millie?" I asked. "It's been quite a day hasn't it?"

"Aye, things are never dull when we're together," Millie replied, smiling back at me. "I'm a wee bit nervy to tell you the truth. I didn't think we'd be speaking on live television tonight!"

"Me neither!" I laughed in response. "We're becoming

quite the celebrities these days, aren't we? Well, you are anyway! You've even got your own memes! They'll be making Millie McCluskey dolls and memorabilia soon!"

"Stop it!" Millie chuckled, giving me a large nudge in the ribs with her elbow.

"Or perhaps even your own jam!" I added with a cheeky smile.

Millie was just about to launch into her best Anthony Joshua impression, with my shoulder in her sights, when our play-fight was interrupted by the sound of Mr Joseph's baritone voice.

"I think we're ready to roll. Look at this…"

Mr Joseph pressed a button on the projector, and suddenly appearing emblazoned onto the façade of the National Gallery was the first slide of our PowerPoint presentation! It was an incredible sight to see this prominent London landmark with our handiwork projected onto the side.

"Ok everyone, we don't have any time to lose," I stated, with an increasing sense of excitement in what we were attempting to do. "Mrs Joseph, are you ready?"

"We are ready to go live," confirmed Mrs Joseph. "In three, two, one…"

# CHAPTER 16

"Action!" shouted Mrs Joseph, as if it was something that she had always wanted to say but had never had the opportunity until now. Millie and I looked at each other for a moment, as if both ushering the other to speak.

"Say something!" whispered Du'ane, who was at that moment kneeling down in front of us holding out a hand held microphone, a bit like one you might find attached to a karaoke machine.

This was the moment. It was now or never!

"Good evening United Kingdom!" I began.

"It isnae the Eurovision Song Contest!" muttered Millie, not exactly helping my nerves. Undeterred, I carried on regardless.

"My name is Peter Lipscombe and this is Millie McCluskey, or as you might know her, the girl who almost fainted on the Queen!" I began. That was payback for the Eurovision comment!

"Earlier today we were being held as prisoners by a criminal organisation called Zolotaya Pantera," Millie said, putting on her best newsreader voice. "We found out some information and fortunately managed to escape. We are going to share that information with you now, in the form of a presentation."

"Please bear with us," I chipped in. "The information you are about to hear may sound fanciful but it is the absolute truth. The reason for us doing this presentation instead of going directly to the police will become clear."

Mrs Joseph panned the camera round to focus on our presentation, projected onto the front of the National Gallery. On the first slide, in massive red letters were the words 'ROBBERY' and 'ART HEIST'.

"As we speak, a well-coordinated robbery is taking place within the buildings of the National Gallery behind us," I announced. "The plan is to steal a great number of world famous and extremely valuable paintings. These will then be removed from the gallery via an underground tunnel that leads to a secret platform on the London Underground, deep beneath Charing Cross Station. These will be loaded onto a train and if something is not done to stop this, they will never be seen again!"

Mr Joseph clicked to move onto the next slide, which read 'ALEKSANDR ZOLOTOV' with a huge picture of the sly and maniacal face of the man himself. It's amazing what you can find on Google! It transpired he is known very well in certain parts of the world as a successful 'businessman'. He had clearly managed to hide certain 'business interests' from the general public, until now!

"This is Aleksandr Zolotov, the owner of Zolotaya Pantera," Millie continued. "What we now know to be one of the largest criminal organisations in the world. He is the man behind all of this, and is somewhere underneath our feet right now!"

The next slide read simply 'DEREK MOONEY', again with a lovely big picture of his miserable, squat features.

"Derek Mooney, the wanted escaped criminal, has been working for this organisation as well," I said. "Earlier today he attempted to attack Millie and to shoot me. In fact, he returned to London specifically to find us."

I hadn't noticed until now, as I was concentrating so hard on speaking to camera, but despite it being the middle of the night, a sizable crowd was beginning to gather around us. This included a couple of other people with cameras who were now filming us. The BBC News

Channel must have been broadcasting the pictures, as there was no way this many people would have turned up! It was working!

"Now you may be wondering why we didn't just go to the police with this information?" said Millie, preparing to drop the most shocking bombshell of all. "We couldn't go to the police, because the Commissioner of the Metropolitan Police is working for Zolotaya Pantera!"

The assembled crowd gasped in shock at this news, as the next slide appeared with the name 'DAME HARRIET RODWELL'.

"For our final big reveal..." I began, now feeling the energy of the crowd more and more, as I brought a greater sense of theatre to my presentation, "...I give you the Home Secretary!"

Again, a huge gasp from the crowd greeted our final slide which read simply 'HENRY MAWDEN-SMYTHE MP'.

"He is also involved and has been paid a lot of money to cover this up," Millie added.

By now the crowd was now several people thick, and there were TV crews from other television stations, trying to manoeuvre around each other to try and get the best possible shot of us and the serious allegations being projected in massive letters for the whole world to see.

"This has gone better than we could have hoped for, but still no sign of the police!" I whispered to Millie so as to not be heard by the microphone. "They will be getting away soon and there will be nothing that can be done about it".

"They may still be in there. Don't give up hope," said Millie. "We've done our bit".

"I've got to admit it Lippy," said Du'ane. "I never thought your plan would have worked so well, but I should never have doubted you."

"It hasn't worked though, has it?" I stated, in a more resigned tone. "All we've done is create a crowd, meanwhile there's a robbery going on."

Just as we were about to pack up everything and sadly accept that our hope to catch these dreadful criminals in the act was a forlorn one, we witnessed a car screech past us at a speed not usually seen in Westminster. The car skidded to a standstill, right next to the main entrance of the predominantly glass-fronted modern National Gallery extension, just outside the Canadian Embassy over to our left. Before any of us could say anything, another car followed! Then another car! Then a van!

"What's going on?" Millie shouted. "This doesn't look like the police. Do you think these are more members of the gang who have come to help them escape?"

"No, I don't think so. This wasn't in the plan that we heard them discuss," I replied. "Everything was intended to be subterranean and out of view. That was the masterplan. Not this."

As we spoke, the car doors began opening in almost a synchronised fashion, and out came around twenty to thirty people, all dressed in dark clothing and what from our vantage point appeared to be body armour. Most noticeably, they were all holding guns. Then from the van appeared another ten or so bodies. Between them, they were carrying a huge battering ram. This was serious stuff!

"They're going to break in!" shouted Du'ane. "This is epic! It's like we're inside a movie!"

The armour-clad group took a small run up before charging at the glass doors. There was a loud smash as glass flew everywhere. Almost immediately the large group disappeared from view and into the National Gallery. The crowd were utterly engrossed in the action, desperate to know what was happening. Part of me wished I was with them. I know it seems like a very strange thing to say, but in a way, I had grown accustomed to the danger. Almost like I'd gotten the taste for it! Me! Little Peter Lipscombe, the quiet skinny boy from rural Cambridgeshire! Now bona fide thrill seeker! Mostly though, I just wanted to finish what I had started and play a part in ensuring the criminals were brought to justice.

By this point Mr Joseph had turned off the projector. Mrs Joseph had handed the camera to another BBC cameraman who had arrived on the scene. Our work here was done. The mission was far from complete but there seemed little more that we could do at this moment in time. As we were packing up our kit, I felt a tap on my shoulder.

"Hello Peter. We meet again."

I turned around and looked up to see a tall gentleman peering back at me. Out of context it took a few moments for me to place his face. Then I realised where I had seen him before. It had been in an interview room at Orsk police station up in Scotland. This was after the plane containing Millie and Derek Mooney had been shot down, when she had been kidnapped by Mooney and his gang. It was this gentleman that had recommended Millie and I receive the George Medal from the Queen. What was he doing here?

"You are making quite a habit of this aren't you?" the well-spoken gentleman said. Looking at Millie, he continued, "I see you have your regular sidekick with you. Thick as thieves you two, aren't you?"

"We come as a team," I replied to the gentleman earnestly, "and if anything, I'm the sidekick. Millie is the *tour de force* in this partnership!"

Millie smiled back at me as I gave a friendly wink in her direction.

"Well that's charming," the gentleman replied, somewhat dismissively. "Anyway, I need you to…"

BANG. BANG. The sound of gunfire filled the air! It was coming from the direction of the National Gallery. Whoever that armed response team were working for, it appeared that they had located our friends from Zolotaya Pantera.

"I need you to come with me now please," the

gentleman continued, "and your friend Millie."

"Hang on a minute!" said Mr Joseph. "They are with us. They are in our care. Their parents will be here soon."

"Ok fine," the gentleman replied. "You had better come with us too".

With that, me, Millie, Du'ane, Mr Joseph and Mrs Joseph were loaded into a small minibus, along with Mr Joseph's expensive projector and equipment.

"Where are we going?" I asked, still in a daze at what was going on.

The gentleman looked at me. "MI5 HQ," he replied, as we sped off at top speed.

# CHAPTER 17

The minibus ride was a little tense. We all sat there silently contemplating the days dramatic events. We found ourselves in a very unusual situation. Looking around at the other familiar faces, and some not so familiar, everyone appeared very tired and I was no exception. It was now approaching 2am following the most exhausting day of my life, and it was only the adrenalin carrying me through by this point. After a short ride, the minibus stopped outside an imposing white building.

"Please disembark," the well-spoken gentleman instructed in a polite yet forceful manner. We duly stepped out of the minibus and surveyed our surroundings. The building was on the banks of the River Thames, close to a bridge.

"Is this the headquarters of MI5?" Millie asked, seeming somewhat awestruck.

"This is Thames House, our headquarters," the gentleman confirmed. "Please follow me."

We followed the gentleman through the large doors into a reception area.

"I'm going to have to ask you to put on blindfolds," the gentleman instructed. "It is nothing to worry about, but of course a lot of very important top-secret work happens here and we can't take any risks."

Now blindfolded, we were led down corridors, into lifts, and finally to our destination.

"You may now remove your blindfolds," the gentleman confirmed. We were in a small room with a table in the middle and two chairs either side. "Peter, Millie – you may take a seat. I'm going to ask your friends to leave for now, but don't worry, they will be in the room next door and will be able to see you and hear you through the glass."

The gentleman pointed to a mirror on the wall. Millie and I looked at the mirror with a look of befuddlement. The gentleman must have noticed, because he explained, "It's a two-way mirror. This is our interrogation room – it's so we can see what's happening inside, but you can't see us. Clever isn't it?"

I nodded back at the gentleman as Du'ane, Mr Joseph and Mrs Joseph were led into the adjacent room.

"So, are we being interrogated?" I asked, as soon as the gentleman sat down at the table facing us.

"Not at all," he smiled. "You are here voluntarily. You can leave at any time."

"It didn't feel voluntary when you herded us into the minibus," Millie replied, a little cheekily.

"I'm sorry about that," the gentleman replied. "However, we don't have too much time. I had to bring you both back here, due to the confidential nature of the discussion we needed to have. Now, do you two have any more questions to ask before we get started? Quickly though, time really isn't on our side!"

"Who are you?" was the first question that flew, almost involuntarily, from my lips. "I mean, I didn't actually ask you when we met before in Orsk."

"It's a fair question," the gentleman replied. "You can call me Bill."

"Is that your real name?" I asked.

"Of course not!" the gentleman replied. "This is MI5! Look, the most important thing that you need to know is that it's our job to ensure the safety of the citizens of the United Kingdom, and I have a very senior role within this organisation."

"I think I'm going to call you Charles," Millie proclaimed. "You seem like a Charles."

"If it pleases you," the gentleman responded, getting a little irked. "Now, I need you to answer some questions for me…"

"Before we do, how do we know we can trust you?" I asked bravely. "If the Commissioner of the Metropolitan Police and the Home Secretary are working with this gang, then how do we know you are not?"

"Very good question!" the gentleman stated, turning to his clearly less senior colleague who was sat silently on the chair next to him. "I like these two!"

After a moment's thought, the gentleman continued, "If they are in involved, it is obviously an unfortunate situation. We report directly to the Home Secretary and have many dealings with Dame Rodwell as well. However, we are working with a special police unit, separate from the Met Police. They were the team that you would have seen enter the National Gallery tonight. Nobody is above the law and if they are guilty of colluding with a criminal gang then I can guarantee you, we will do all in our power to bring them to justice."

"Ok," I replied, "that's enough for me. Let's talk."

"Thank you, Peter," the gentleman said, sounding relieved to be getting somewhere at last. "You two made some pretty bold statements on that rather impressive PowerPoint projection of yours, which as you can imagine is going to get a lot of people talking. I trust that you would not have resorted to such a stunt if you felt you could go to the police, but as a consequence we need to move fast. By that I mean tonight, as if we wait until tomorrow, the criminals will have had chance to 'clear up their mess.' So, tell me what happened today and what you found out."

Millie and I once again recounted the events of the day. This time though, in intricate detail. From the moment that Mooney had approached and grabbed Millie at

Waterloo Station to the moment that we had hopped into the minibus to take us to MI5, leaving out no detail at all. I was particularly proud of how impressed the gentleman and his colleague looked at our various endeavours, most notably outfoxing Derek Mooney on not one but two occasions, and successfully despatching Zolotov's giant bodyguards. After we had finished our recital, we waited on tenterhooks whilst the gentleman finished taking notes.

"Well, I have to say," the gentleman began, "that you two should really seriously consider a career in espionage! Are you sure you're both only thirteen years old? What you have managed to do, both today and in Orsk is quite incredible! I would give you both a job now if I were allowed to, but unfortunately the laws of this country prevent us from doing so. Nonetheless, I'm quite happy to make you a conditional offer to join our graduate scheme after you've both been to university."

"A conditional offer?" Millie asked. "Conditional on what?"

"Well, conditional on you both still being alive by then!" the gentleman half-joked. "You're not exactly good at staying clear of danger, are you?"

I couldn't disagree with that statement!

"Well, we've told you what we know," I said, cheekily changing the subject. "Now it's only fair if you return the favour!"

The gentleman smiled again. I think it's fair to stay that he admired our enthusiasm!

"Well, there are some things that I can't tell you for national security reasons, but you certainly deserve some answers after the day you've had," the gentleman said, acquiescing to my request for information. "You will already know about Operation Phoenix, which was all about trying to stop a supply of illegal pharmaceuticals entering the United Kingdom and finding those responsible. Well, you two managed to solve that one by yourselves up in Scotland! However, although we caught a number of those responsible, including your friend Derek Mooney, he was as high up in the chain as we managed to get. We couldn't find any further information about who he was working for."

"Until now!" Millie said triumphantly.

"Exactly, until now!" the gentleman underlined. "This is where it gets really interesting though. We had been working on a different mission – Operation Griffin. We like mythical creatures, clearly! Anyway, Operation Griffin was focused on a number of UK businesses being purchased by one particular foreign investor. Nothing unusual there, you would think. However, there was a remarkable similarity to what was happening each time. The investor would try and spot businesses in financial trouble, and offer them loans at a variable rate to 'help' them. Then they would increase the rate on the loans, forcing the businesses to the verge of bankruptcy, before swooping in to buy the companies. Questionable practice, yes, but not necessarily illegal."

"I'm lost!" Millie said. I had to say I felt the same way. What did this have to do with anything?

"Well, these businesses were all in different parts of the country," the gentleman continued. "This was all strategically planned to make it hard to spot the pattern. However, we did in fact, through months of painstaking work manage to solve the puzzle. The businesses were individually perfectly innocent, but if combined, you would have everything you need to make bombs and weaponry."

"Illegal arms traders!" I exclaimed in acknowledgement.

"We think so," the gentleman said. "Or maybe worse. We're not exactly sure yet. The point is, all of these businesses were bought by a company registered in the UK as 'Golden Venture Holdings'. Some further digging revealed that it is the same company that bought the harbour on Orsk. Golden Venture Holdings, as you've probably guessed are a subsidiary of…"

"Zolotaya Pantera!" Millie and I shouted back in

unison.

"Exactly!" the gentleman confirmed. "Zolotaya Pantera, registered in Sochi, Russia. So, all of this, the illegal pharmaceuticals, the illegal arms trading and now this art heist at the National Gallery, all link back to one man – Aleksandr Zolotov! And he's here, somewhere in London as we speak!"

We had seen enough to know that Zolotov was bad news, but this was on a whole new scale.

"Is there anything else we can do to help catch him?" I asked. I was desperate to stop this evil man from further expanding his global organisation of terror.

"I'm sorry to ask any more of you. I know you've already had a very long and emotional day," the gentleman replied. "But yes. I need you to take us to his underground headquarters!"

# CHAPTER 18

Millie and I glanced at each other. She looked a little unsure and I certainly wasn't expecting to be returning to the scene of our earlier shocking discovery and subsequent capture and great escape. At least not quite so soon.

"Of course, we can't force you to come with us," the gentleman stated. "However, you two both know exactly where we need to look. Time spent trying to find where we need to go is time wasted in trying to locate Zolotov, Mooney and the others. We will be with a highly skilled and specially trained armed police unit. I can't promise you both it is without risk though, so you may want a moment to discuss. I will step outside and give you a minute to talk."

With that, the gentleman and his colleague left Millie and I alone in the interview room.

"What do you think Millie?" I asked. "If you don't want to do this I understand. We've taken far too many risks already today."

"Aye, that we have!" Millie agreed. "But we have to see this through to the bitter end now. We've come so far! Just think of all the lives we could save and crime we could prevent if we manage to catch Mooney and Zolotov."

I wasn't surprised any more by Millie's bravery. We had both come a long way from when we first met. What happened to the nervous, introverted boy and cheeky, rough around the edges island girl? Now we were Peter

Lipscombe and Millie McCluskey, brave and fearless secret agents!

"Have you come to a decision?" the gentleman asked on re-entering the room.

"We're ready!" I answered boldly. "Let's go now!"

"Certainly!" said the gentleman. "That was nothing less than I expected from you two!"

As we wandered out of the room, once again being led on our way blindfolded, my thoughts turned to the Josephs. I had been so focused on our dialogue with the gentleman from MI5, I had almost forgotten that the Josephs were in the next room watching this all play out.

"Where are the Josephs?" I asked. "Will they be ok?"

"I think we'll be fine," came the reply from a familiar voice. It was Du'ane! "Don't worry, we're coming as well! As soon as my dad heard the plan, he insisted he would only let you agree to it if we could tag along!"

"I don't want you to put yourselves in danger on my account," I stated. "This is mine and Millie's battle. We are the ones whose lives have been impacted by these terrible people."

"Nonsense!" replied Du'ane adamantly. "I wouldn't miss this for the world. Besides, you heard what they said. We've got a crack team of armed police officers with us. What could possibly go wrong?"

I had learnt the hard way where that particular phrase usually got you. In my experience, into a whole heap of trouble! I had to agree though that this time the odds were at least stacked heavily in our favour.

We were led out of the building into the London night air. As our blindfolds were removed, a solitary fox skipped past in front of us. My dad always said that seeing a fox walk past on its own was a good omen. At this moment, I desperately hoped he was right. We were loaded back into the minibus once again and sat waiting whilst the gentleman from MI5 took a phone call.

"Peter, we don't have to do this," Mr Joseph said,

sensing a modicum of trepidation amongst the gathering. "I know this is important, but not more important than your wellbeing. I'm already wondering how I can even begin to explain all this to your parents as it is!"

"Mr Joseph, we have to do this," I replied. "If we are not able to find Mooney and Zolotov, then Millie and I will constantly be looking over our shoulders. We need to end this now!"

Out of the window, we could see the gentleman end his phone call. He clambered on board the minibus, sliding the door shut as he took his seat. The minibus set off at a good speed on the virtually empty roads.

"Well, I'll start with the good news," he began. "That was the police superintendent from the special unit. They have managed to prevent any of the paintings from being stolen from the National Gallery! All because of you two and your endeavour and perseverance. Hundreds of priceless works saved from falling into the wrong hands."

"Yes!" shouted Millie and I simultaneously, giving each other a huge high five. Mission accomplished! It felt incredible to know that was all because of us. Well, I mean the armed police unit helped of course, but you know what I mean!

"We have apprehended many members of the criminal gang and taken them into custody," the gentleman continued. "We have also arrested Harriet Rodwell and Henry Mawden-Smythe MP. Officers are currently searching their houses and offices as we speak. Lots of good news, but…"

Why is there always a but? I got the feeling this was going to be something we didn't want to hear!

"…unfortunately, there is no sign of Mooney or Zolotov."

I half-expected that this would be the case.

"Might they be hiding at their headquarters?" Millie asked.

"It's a longshot," the gentleman replied, "as they know

that is likely to be the first place we would look. However, even if not, hopefully we can find some clues as to their whereabouts."

In a matter of moments, the minibus pulled up outside Charing Cross Station. Large crowds and television crews were still gathered outside the National Gallery. Now, rather than watching us and our amateur broadcast, they were watching a stream of gang members being loaded one by one into police vans. A satisfying sight! However, our work was not yet done for the night. We alighted the minibus and entered the station, flanked to the front and rear by our armed guard.

We were shown as far as the publicly accessible underground platform by a station security guard. Then it was over to us. Millie typed in the code that she had used earlier – 01806. To our great surprise it had not been changed and the door was opened instantaneously! Zolotov may be some kind of criminal mastermind, but that was a sloppy mistake. I could only presume that he had left that particular task to Derek Mooney – which as our experience had shown, was perhaps not the best idea!

We once again made our way down the steps, arriving at the secret platform. This time though we had the additional protection of our entourage.

"Follow me everyone," called Millie, who was clearly revelling in this role. "The door to Zolotov's headquarters is this way!"

We wandered down the platform. Once again, the code to the door had not been changed. This had all seemed suspiciously easy. I had at least expected that we would have to break down a couple of the doors. Perhaps a controlled explosion here and there. Somewhat disappointingly there had been no pyrotechnics required at all! Very strange!

"Could this be a trap?" I asked the gentleman from MI5. "This has all been way too easy so far. I'm not sure we should enter that door. I have a bad feeling about this."

"We have to be alive to that possibility of course," the gentleman replied. "You do not have to stay with us, if you don't want to. You have more than played your part and we can take it from here."

"No, we want to stay!" shouted Millie enthusiastically. "Finish what we started. Don't we Peter?"

"Yes, we want to stay," I responded without hesitation. "I just think we need to be really cautious, that's all."

"That's fine," the gentleman stated. "These officers are some of the best trained in the country, if not the world, at handling situations like this. They will go in first, sweep the place, and if it's safe we will follow in afterwards."

"You know what you're doing," I replied, feeling much more reassured.

With that, six of the police unit pounded in through the door, fearlessly prepared to face whatever lied in wait for them. Millie and I were left on the platform with the Josephs, the gentleman and his colleague from MI5, and two further police officers. There was a tense silence, all of us expecting to hear some kind of commotion coming from beyond the door, but nothing. A minute or so passed. I looked around the platform, still scarcely believing where we were or what was happening.

The silence was broken by a quiet scraping or scuttling sound coming from the rail tracks. I presumed it was a rat. As nobody else had appeared to hear this sound, I took a couple of steps towards the tracks. Suddenly and without warning, a man leapt up from beyond the edge of the platform, propelling himself with surprising agility onto the edge of the platform and landing on both feet. It took me a moment or two to register what was happening. I drew my eyes up and focused on the man's face. It was our old adversary Derek Mooney, and he was pointing a gun directly at me!

# CHAPTER 19

"Nobody move or I'm going to redecorate the platform with the boy's brains," Mooney shouted with his trademark sneer.

I stayed as still as a statue, my heart beating faster than I ever imagined it could. Out of the corner of my eye, I noticed that the two police officers both had their guns trained on Mooney. We were now in the midst of an armed standoff.

"Now Derek, please don't do anything stupid," the gentleman from MI5 said in a remarkably calm fashion. "Put the gun down and we can talk about things. We can even let you go, if that's what you want. Just please stop pointing the gun at the young man and we can discuss things rationally."

"No chance!" shouted back Mooney, sounding somewhat maniacal. "The moment I lower this gun, you'll shoot me. I know how this works. Now, back off – this is between me and the boy. I don't want to hear anyone's voice except the boy. Do you understand?"

Everyone nodded frantically, keen not to enrage Mooney further. Mooney turned to me and stared deep into my eyes, without blinking once. His was a look of pure rage, the like of which I hadn't experienced before in my thirteen years on this planet.

"I just want to know," began Mooney, "why it is that you have decided to ruin my life? I was happy up in

Scotland. I had a job that I liked on a lovely little island. I lived in a castle, for gawds sake! I had prospects. I had power. I had control. I was running the whole operation for one of the biggest and best companies in the world. Yes, what we were doing was illegal, but was it hurting anyone really?"

"What about the men you kept as prisoners? Like my dad!" Millie shouted out, unable to contain her emotions any longer.

"Did I not say be quiet?" Mooney screamed as he pointed his gun towards the ceiling and fired. The deafening sound of the gunfire echoed around the cavernous tunnels, as dust and tiles dropped to the ground, narrowly missing the Josephs. "Next time, that'll be you, you interfering ginger nuisance! I should have gotten rid of both you and your wretched father when I had the chance!"

Millie was clearly shaken at being shouted at in such a way, especially by a clearly unhinged man holding a gun. She was now noticeably shaking, as an involuntary tear slid down her pale, freckly cheek to the floor.

"As I was saying before being so rudely interrupted," Mooney continued, his face gradually becoming redder and redder, "things were going pretty well for me, and then along came Peter Lipscombe, poking around in all sorts of things that didn't concern him. Causing trouble for me and Zolotov, just because he decided to be nosey! Now, look at me! Look at me! Everything I worked so hard for up in Scotland – gone! Living in a castle – gone! Then prison! I swore never to return to that place, but this time was worse than ever. Being taunted by all the other inmates because the people that put me there happened to be a pair of children!"

Mooney was shouting loudly by this point. Just when you thought his voice could not get any louder, he found a whole new decibel level.

"Then I finally managed to escape from prison!"

Mooney said, resuming his unchallenged soliloquy. "I thought things were finally going my way. My plan was to come to London, exact some kind of revenge on you pathetic kids, get one last huge payday from this art heist, and escape the country to who knows where. Brazil? Portugal? Abu flaming Dhabi? I didn't care. Somewhere hot that I could disappear to and start a new life. Instead what do I end up with? Being given the run-around yet again by a pair of teenagers! Losing my little finger! Then just to top it all off, you ruin the plan that was going to be my retirement fund! What do you have to say for yourselves?"

I didn't really want to say anything. I didn't know what I could say to help the situation in any way. Clearly Mooney wanted me to say something though, or why insist that it is only me to speak?

"I'm sorry?" I said tentatively. "It's nothing personal. It really isn't. You work for the gang that killed my best friend Finny. I just want justice and to stop you all before anyone else gets hurt."

"My best friend! Before anyone else gets hurt! Wah, wah, wah," Mooney repeated back to me, mimicking my voice in a child-like manner pretending to cry, before bursting out laughing to himself. Hysterical laughter. Sickening laughter, that echoed loudly.

"I'm sorry," Mooney continued, after composing himself. "Actually, I really am sorry. You see, it was me that forced your friend's car off the road. I wasn't trying to kill him. It was his old man that I was after. Your friend's death – well, that was just a happy accident! Ha ha!"

I wanted to shout so badly. I wanted to cry and scream. The man standing before me was the very man responsible for killing my best friend. Here he was happily admitting it and seemingly taking great pleasure from the misery he had caused to Finny's family, to me and to many others. However, I didn't cry. I didn't scream or shout. I just stared deeply into Mooney's eyes. I was not going to give him the reaction he was after.

At that moment I heard the start of a rumbling, seemingly coming from the tunnel. It surely couldn't be an underground train at this time of night though? It was now past 3am. The sound very quickly got louder and louder, very much like the start of a small earthquake. Mooney looked confused. His concentration had noticeably wavered. He was still pointing the gun directly at me, but his manic laughter had turned into a sort of frantic energy. His eye twitched nervously. The sound was now loud enough to drown out any conversation, and whatever was making the noise would surely be upon us any moment.

Just then, for reasons that we will never find out, Mooney took a step backwards as if to back away from the guns of the police officers trained on him. His back foot reached beyond the edge of the platform and for what must have been a moment, but seemed like an age, Mooney teetered perilously on the edge of the platform trying to retain his balance. It was to no avail though, as he went toppling backwards off the edge, falling onto the tracks below and dropping his gun in the process.

At that moment, a train appeared from the tunnel at the far end of the platform. The train was hurtling along at great speed, without the remotest intention of stopping at the platform. The driver evidently spotted Mooney lying on the track, as he must have immediately attempted to slam on the brakes. I'm not sure if you've ever heard the sound of a train attempting to brake suddenly whilst going far too quickly? Well I can tell you, it's the most piercing screech you can ever imagine, and not a sound that any of us there present on that platform will ever be able to forget.

I put my hands in front of my eyes as the train inevitably failed to stop in time for poor Derek Mooney. His story was not to have a happy ending, but an ending it most certainly did have. Right there and then. Not the nicest way to leave this world, but I'm sad to say, it was hard to argue that he deserved any better.

The train gradually slowed, until it almost came to a standstill. However, much to the surprise of those of us gathered on the secret platform, the train began to pick up pace again. I took my hands away from eyes just in time to see a face that I recognised staring back at me from on board the train. It was none other than Aleksandr Zolotov himself! He caught my gaze and looked me straight in the eye. I couldn't be completely sure, but I'm sure I noticed a small grin appear on his chiselled features as the train disappeared from view.

"Peter, Millie!" exclaimed the gentleman from MI5 rushing towards us. "Are you both alright?"

Millie and I stared at each other, our faces sharing the same vacant expression. Two people so completely in shock at their ordeal, twinned with the gradual realisation that it might be over. I looked over at the gentleman and attempted something close to a nod of the head.

"Peter, Millie, Du'ane, Mr and Mrs Joseph," the gentleman continued, addressing us all directly. "I think it's best that you leave this area immediately. This is police business now."

We were led immediately back through the door to the secret platform. We wearily climbed the steps for the last time and made our way back up to ground level. We stood for a moment on the concourse in front of Charing Cross Station trying to process what had just happened. After a few seconds, Millie walked over and threw her arms around me. We both began to cry as the realisation of the danger we had just escaped from sank in.

Millie and I remained there for several minutes, hugging each other tightly. It began to rain lightly, but that didn't register with either of us. We were both safe and neither ourselves, nor our family and friends, would have to worry about Derek Mooney ever again.

# CHAPTER 20

It was a beautiful sunny Friday morning in Little Dunham, right in the heart of rural Cambridgeshire. The wind was whistling gently through the branches of the tall trees that surrounded the quaint churchyard in the middle of my home village. Millie and I sat on a wooden bench, enjoying a moment of silence and contemplation. I looked over at Millie as the sun glistened off her long red hair. The sheer peace and serenity of the moment offered a sharp contrast to our chaotic trip to London the previous weekend.

The week had been almost perfect. We started off with a couple of well-earned rest days on Monday and Tuesday. We hosted the McCluskeys at our home and enjoyed time in the house and garden, playing games and talking. Monday was mainly spent recounting and reliving our weekend adventures and traumas with our long-suffering parents. I think it's fair to say that my mother would prefer it if we had chosen a different hobby to tracking down international criminal gangs, but thankfully her relief at having me back with her in one piece fairly swiftly replaced her initial anger at my 'reckless behaviour'.

Tuesday began in the most bizarre fashion. My dad's newspaper arrived as always through the letterbox. He went to collect it, but rather than take it off to his study to arrange it into piles after detaching the various supplements, he took one look at it and shouted out, "Peter and Millie! You had better come and have a look at this!"

We raced over to my dad who handed us the newspaper with the front page showing. Staring back at us were our own faces, with the huge headline PLUCKY TEENAGERS FOIL ATTEMPTED ART HEIST.

"You're making quite a habit of appearing in the media, aren't you?" my dad said, laughing away. "At this rate you'll be hiring a manager to look after your public appearances!"

As Millie and I sat in our lounge reading the article out loud to our parents, the whole thing still seemed so surreal. Had we really done all of this? As exciting as it was to see our faces in a national newspaper, a small part of me was longing for my old life back. To subtly slide back into the mundane normality of Athletics Club, watching pointless clips on YouTube and playing far too much FIFA on the PlayStation. The celebrity game definitely wasn't for me – I loved my quiet village life too much.

Wednesday and Thursday had been spent doing some more low-key tourism. I decided to show Millie the sights and sounds of our local area. I wanted her to see the places that really meant something to me, in the same way that she had taken me around her wonderful island. On Wednesday we took a bus to our nearest town, Ely, and I showed her the Cathedral that had been the setting for Finny's funeral. We visited Oliver Cromwell's House and took a little boat trip down the river. On Thursday, we went for a wander around the village and we walked past my old primary school and the field where my Athletics Club train. We also called in to visit Finny's parents. It was amazing to see Millie and Captain Finn meet in person for the first time. We were even treated to a good hour of Captain Finn's legendary anecdotes!

However, none of these experiences or locations meant as much to me as the place we were sat at that very moment. I would come here at least once a week, often more, to sit on this bench right in front of Finny's final resting place. Sometimes I would just sit here in silence so I could feel close to him. At other times, I would tell him about my day or how the school football team was doing. I'm not sure why, but it always made me feel better afterwards. Today was particularly special, as I could share the moment with Millie.

"I love it here," Millie said, smiling softly at me. "It's so beautiful and peaceful. Thank you for showing me Finny's grave. I wish I had known him. He must have been so special to you."

"He was. He is," I responded wistfully. "He always will be."

"When you're here, what do you talk to him about?" Millie asked.

"Whatever comes into my head," I replied. "Sometimes I say a lot. Sometimes not so much. Just anything that I think he would want to know. Why don't you say hello?"

"Really?" Millie replied, a little anxiously. "I didn't even know him."

"Any friend of mine, will be a friend of his, trust me," I said. "You and Finny are so alike in many ways. You would have gotten on incredibly."

"Ok, if you're sure," Millie continued. "Hello Finny. It's nice to meet you. I'm Millie. Sorry if you cannae understand me. I'm not from round these parts you see. Wherever you are right now, you're probably worrying about your wee friend Peter. Well, you dinnae need to. I'm going to take good care of him."

Millie smiled at me again and reached out her hand, which I took in mine. Something felt so natural about holding Millie's hand. It made me feel somehow safer, like an invisible forcefield was protecting us both. I smiled back warmly.

"Thank you, Millie," I said. "You probably feel this is all a little strange, but it really helps me."

"I think it's lovely," she replied. "You are such a good friend Peter Lipscombe. To Finny and to me."

We stayed for a few more minutes and I told Finny all about our adventures and misadventures in London. Lastly, I told him about Derek Mooney's unfortunate but unquestionably deserved demise at the hands of an underground train.

As we stood up to leave, I turned to Finny's grave one final time and muttered softly under my breath, "Now, Finny. Now, you can rest in peace my friend."

We took a slow walk back to my house. As Millie and I chatted, my mind wandered a little. Millie and her family were due to fly back to Scotland that evening. It would be so hard to say goodbye to Millie once again. Yes, we had WhatsApp video calls, but it wasn't quite the same as having your partner in crime by your side to share the little moments of magic that life delivers. However, something told me that there would be many more shared adventures to come!

"We're home!" I shouted to alert my parents, as Millie and I burst through the front door. As we leapt clear of the pile of presumably recently delivered post, something unusual caught my eye. I bent down to pick the post up, and right at the top of the pile was a colourful postcard featuring scenes from a mysterious faraway place. Millie and I stared open-mouthed in shock and amazement as we simultaneously read the slogan on the front of the postcard, 'GREETINGS FROM SOCHI, RUSSIA.'

"What does it say on the back?" Millie asked anxiously.

I tentatively turned over the postcard to read the short, scribbled message on the reverse. The message read:

*Dear Peter and Millie,*

*Congratulations on winning the battle. The war, however, rages on.*

*Until we meet again…*

*AZ.*

"AZ!" I exclaimed. "Aleksandr Zolotov!"

Millie and I looked at each other. We knew exactly what this meant. As I suspected, our adventures were to be far from over.

# ABOUT THE AUTHOR

Sam Bartram was born in Nottingham and lives in beautiful rural Norfolk, England, with his wife and two children. When he is not writing, Sam enjoys running, walking, singing, watching sport (particularly Norwich City FC), travelling, theatre, film and spending time with his friends and family.

Sam loves to hear from readers and will always try to reply to questions and messages. You can contact Sam via:

**Facebook:**
www.facebook.com/sambartramauthor

**Twitter:**
@sbartramauthor

# PETER AND MILLIE ADVENTURES

Books available in the series:

1. FINNY'S STAR

2. UNDERGROUND ESCAPADE

Printed in Great Britain
by Amazon